HORROR

PANIC STATION

by
Stephen Bowkett
and illustrated by Joanna Roberts

HENDERSON
An imprint of DK Publishing, Inc.
Copyright © 1996 Dorling Kindersley Ltd.

To Andrew Holmes,
the real father of Roy Case,
and to all my friends in
The Monsters Club
who understand
the sweet music of the night.

Chapter 1

The small group of explorers made their way carefully through the burned-out city. Although the Mutant Wars were just about over, small bands of monsters still inhabited the smashed shells of buildings, hiding in ambush for human survivors.

Mark, who was leading the team, held up his hand for the others to stop. They trusted Mark's instincts as completely as he did himself. And now, as the cool wind changed direction and brought a smell of sour ashes, there was suddenly a tension in the air.

And more than a tension. A danger…

Gary moved up close to his friend. The boys were just fourteen years old, but the horrors of war had washed the innocence from their faces. Now they had the look of all Normals on Earth; shocked, angry, determined that such a thing would never happen on this planet again.

"Trouble?" Gary wondered. He silently drew his Laserbolt gun from the leather holster at his side, holding it in readiness for battle. His long, dark hair was tied back from his eyes with a scrap of blue rag: Mark's fair hair, equally long, was knotted with a leather thong.

He nodded without wasting words to confirm the inevitable. In the ruins of Earth's once proud cities, there was always trouble to be found.

Mark lifted his Power Scimitar and pointed it unwaveringly toward the crumbled wreckage of a skyscraper.

"I smell them," he whispered, turning away to glance at the frightened group of youngsters they were trying to guide toward the coast and safety. "Reptiloids, the worst kind. I think we'd better get the others back behind cover."

He was looking at Gary as he said this, and saw his friend's face change – rage suddenly replacing concern.

Then there came the searing, sizzling blast of Gary's Laserbolt gun firing, the dazzling beam whisking past his ear.

Mark whirled around.

A huge, gray-skinned Reptiloid with evil-looking red stripes along its flanks was hurtling down toward him, its huge jaws agape, and…

A curtain of static filled the computer screen and Mark was suddenly back inside his bedroom, his mind whirling as he wondered what had happened. He pressed the reset button on the machine, but the blizzard of static remained. This had never happened before, and he had no idea what to do about it.

After a few seconds' thought, Mark decided the best thing was to call Gary, who knew more about computers than any other kid in the school – more than any other kid in Kenniston, most likely.

Mark swore once, with feeling, at his computer, then left it, still flickering crazily, as he headed for the door.

His mother, Sarah Watkins, was coming up the stairs as Mark reached the landing. She looked worried.

4

"Is the TV out, too?" Mark wondered. The weather had been changeable during the past few days, and it seemed as though a storm was brewing. So maybe the problem was atmospherics, static in the air itself.

Mrs. Watkins looked at her son. She seemed close to tears.

"Tina's not back...She said she'd be home by five."

"Perhaps...," Mark began. Mrs. Watkins continued: "I called the modeling agency and they said her assignment was at MZTV..."

"The new cable TV station," Mark said. He'd heard about it at school. "She probably had to stay on late to finish the shoot."

Tina Watkins, four years older than Mark, wanted to become an actress. An agency had taken her onto their books, and landed her occasional modeling jobs and bit parts in TV ads, which earned her some money while she applied for a place in drama school. She often rolled in late, Mark recalled.

But Sarah Watkins was shaking her head, and now the tears came, quivering in her eyes and spilling over onto her cheeks.

"I phoned the TV station," she explained, "and they said – Oh, Mark, I'm so worried something's happened!"

"What did they say, Mom?"

Mark went down the stairs and put his arm around his mother's shoulder.

"They said...," she sobbed, then swallowed hard to control her fear. "They told me that Tina left hours ago…"

☠

Police Officer Baxter was very understanding, and his gentle, friendly attitude helped to calm Sarah Watkins's concerns.

Mark made some coffee and brought it into the living room, just as his mother was explaining how hard it was to cope sometimes, since her husband had left over four years ago now.

Mark frowned and irritation burned up through him. He hated Mom talking like this, especially to strangers. But it was as though she had to talk to somebody – anybody, to help deal with the pain. Mark just wished she'd talk to him more. Or, better still, meet someone else who'd take her mind off Dad.

Mark caught the officer's eye and the man smiled.

"Mrs. Watkins," Baxter said, interrupting her, "even if your husband were here, there would be nothing he could do. Kenniston's a big city, and no way could he, or even the whole family, hope to cover that much ground."

"But I feel so helpless sitting, doing nothing!"

"Of course you do, but it's best if you stay by the telephone, to be here when we call back – or if your daughter calls. Nine times out of ten, there's a perfectly ordinary, simple explanation for this kind of thing."

But what about the tenth time? The thought

flashed through Mark's mind but he said nothing: he poured the coffee instead.

Officer Baxter was explaining that the usual procedure was to put out an APB on anyone suspected of having been abducted.

"That's an All Points Bulletin," Mark said. He grinned. "I love to watch all the cop shows on TV!"

Baxter grinned back at him. "Right on, son. An APB, Mrs. Watkins, means we circulate a description of your daughter, and her last known whereabouts, to all our patrol cars. Several hundred police officers will be on the lookout for Tina. The only question is whether we'll find her before she comes home by herself!"

Sarah seemed reassured, so that Baxter felt able to leave ten minutes later. Mark saw him to the door.

"Take care of your mom," the man said. He pushed his police cap a little higher on his head and squinted up into the sky. The sun was close to setting, deep red light spilling through ragged, overcast clouds in the west. Mark thought it was an odd sky, somehow menacing.

"Of course I will," Mark answered. Now – and he'd never noticed this before – he felt an eerie metallic tingling on his tongue. It was as though electricity were creeping into the air, lending it an unpleasant dryness.

Baxter glanced at the boy and knew that he'd be as good as his word. He nodded, smiled thinly, then walked through the gathering gloom toward the patrol car parked at the end of the driveway.

Back inside the house, Sarah had started one of her "cleaning sprees". She did this now and then – cleaning the house, dusting, washing pots, to take her mind off painful thoughts.

"Need any help, Mom?" Mark asked, but he knew she didn't. For a while at least, she needed just to be busy.

"I'm okay. You go back upstairs and play with your computer."

Officer Baxter's arrival had taken Mark's mind off the computer entirely. But now, as he climbed the stairs, he remembered how the screen had gone down, ruining the game, and his intention to call Gary about it.

As Mark approached his bedroom, he heard the familiar, annoying hiss of the static…but also something else. Voices. Whispery, ceaseless voices, many of them, all talking together.

He inched around the half-open door.

The computer screen blazed at him like some weird, insane white eye. And reflected there, coming and going like dreams, were scores of ghostly faces.

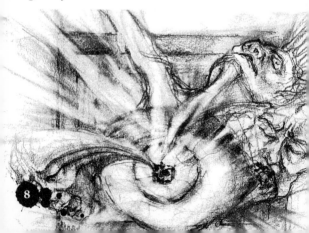

Chapter 2

"Yeah, I've had the same problem," Gary Swann said as Mark explained the trouble with his computer. "Except I was playing *Nemesis Pit* instead of *Mutant Wars*. Reached level thirty now," he added smugly, knowing that Mark had only ever made it to level nineteen.

Mark smiled as he waited for Gary to finish boasting – not that Mark would ever accuse him of being simply a big head. As well as being a genius when it came to understanding computers, Gary was a wizard at playing any game you cared to mention. And that was not just at school: Gary's machine was connected to the Internet through a phone line, which meant he could battle against other game players all across the country. There was a rumor that Gary Swann was among the top one hundred in the nationwide computer battle *Shadow Swarm*, and that he played for three or four hours every evening when he got home. These days, Mark usually only got to see him on weekends.

"So you think it might be the strange weather we're having?" Mark said, bringing Gary back to the point. Even now, as Mark stood in the hallway staring at the front door, he could see distant flares of lightning through the frosted glass panels, while down the phone line came the crackly, faraway spitting sound of the storm.

"No doubt about it," Gary agreed. "And as you can hear, it's affecting the telephone network, too.

I've been getting all kinds of weird stuff on my computer screen from the Net."

"What stuff?" Mark wondered, thinking back to the odd faces he'd seen earlier, upon entering his bedroom…

Or *thought* he'd seen. The faces had disappeared an instant later, leaving the screen slashed across with electric snow, and nothing else.

"Unusual interference – oh, moving figures, staring eyes, like some kind of old horror movie was trying to play through the telephone system. Never seen anything like it. But we live in strange times, Mark old buddy. Strange times."

Mark found Gary's comments unnerving rather than reassuring. He mentioned the fact that Tina hadn't come home yet, and how the police had come around to get details.

Gary went very quiet.

"Hello – you still there?" Mark spoke into the soft hissing coming from the receiver. "Gary?"

"Still here," Gary said. His voice sounded strained, as though there were something he knew about, but was holding back from saying. "Um, listen, Mark…"

"What is it – well, come on!" Mark snapped, as Gary hesitated.

"It's funny you should mention Tina disappearing. The guys on the 'Net – the other kids playing *Shadow Swarm* – they've been talking about people vanishing over the past couple of weeks."

"What, not coming home?"

"Not turning up *anywhere*," Gary went on.

10

"And Leila was telling me there are two people at her school who're missing."

"Well, that makes me feel lots better!"

"I'm only trying to help," Gary answered. He could hear the concern in his best friend's voice, and wished now he'd never brought the subject up, especially the part about the two students from his sister's school. They'd been about Tina's age, and so far the police had found no trace of them.

"Well, you're not helping!" Mark felt his temper rising and made an effort to control it. None of this was Gary's fault, and like Gary said, he'd only been trying to put Mark in the picture.

"I'm sorry, Gary." The apology was swift and sincere. "I'm just getting myself in a state about it all. The cops will probably find her before long, right?"

"Probably tonight." Gary wondered if Mark could hear the hollowness in his voice. The two girls Leila knew had been missing for two weeks already.

"Where can all these people be vanishing to?" Mark went on, glancing up as distant thunder made the front door rattle.

Gary said, "Well, we know where they're vanishing *from*. From what I can gather, all the missing persons disappeared in Kenniston. And –"

"And what?"

Gary swallowed hard. "And I was about to say, why don't you come over in the morning? Bring your bike. If Tina's not back, we can cruise round and look for her. At least you'll feel like you're doing something."

Mark considered for a moment.

"Okay, I'll do that. Mrs. Dayne from next door has come by. She's with Mom now. I'm sure she won't mind keeping Mom company tomorrow."

"That's settled, then. And Leila will be here, too," Gary added, knowing that Mark had a soft spot for her.

Mark smiled at his friend's mischief.

"See you tomorrow then. And thanks, Gary."

He put the telephone down and leaned around the living room door to tell his mother he was turning in for the night. Sarah Watkins was red-eyed, but had stopped crying now. That made Mark feel a little better.

He went upstairs and walked across to the window, opened it, and gazed out.

The wind had strengthened and came whooshing through the trees in the nearby gardens, up into Mark's face. The sting of electricity still tingled in his nostrils. Way beyond the trees and the quiet suburbs lay the city center. That's where the storm seemed to be building, as lightning flashed and tangled through the low clouds hanging above the glowing skyline of office buildings.

One unexpectedly bright flash made Mark flinch. He closed the window, then undressed and switched on his bedside lamp. The bulb faded and brightened – and over on Mark's desk, the computer – which was switched off now – gave a single sharp *snap*, as tiny tendrils of blue light skittered over the screen.

Mark waited for something else to happen. But

nothing did.

He flipped through a comic book for ten minutes, but found his attention wandering. So he turned out his light and lay in the darkness, waiting for sleep to come.

Chapter 3

Leila Swann had the same bright, open face as her brother, and the same fine, dark hair, though she wore hers very long, almost down to her waist. The look of concern in her eyes as she answered the door to Mark triggered sudden tears in his, and brought fresh worries about Tina's safety.

"Oh Mark, I'm so sorry this has happened…"

Mark was embarrassed enough to be almost crying in front of her – but now his embarrassment doubled as she stepped onto the porch and hugged him. In the hallway, Gary grinned at his sister's show of sympathy and at the red flush spreading quickly across his friend's face.

"Let the boy alone, Lee," he called jovially. "I've lost count of how many of my pals you've scared off like this!"

"How would you like it," Leila snapped back, turning to her brother, "if *I* vanished mysteriously?"

"At least it would be quiet around the house for a change."

"Come on in, Mark," Leila said, ignoring Gary's comment. " He's upset, too, you know, but making stupid jokes is the only way he can cope with it."

"Yeah," Mark said, managing to summon a weak smile. "Thanks. I mean, to both of you. If you guys weren't around – well, don't know what I'd do."

Leila led Mark into the kitchen. The table was

cluttered with breakfast things, which Mrs. Swann was clearing away. She looked up as the three entered and asked Mark about his sister.

"There's no word," he explained, struggling to force back another wave of anxiety. "Sergeant Baxter stopped by earlier. He couldn't promise that nothing was wrong, but he said that at least Tina hadn't been found – you know – dead."

"How's your mother?" Mrs. Swann wondered. Her eyes, too, were shiny with tears. "Is there anything I can do to help?"

Mark shrugged. "It's okay. Mrs. Dayne came over again first thing. She brought some groceries and says she'll hang around to keep Mom company. Mom said I ought to get out of the house and take my mind off it: just worrying was doing nobody any good…'Course, *she'll* just sit there and worry about it!" Mark flashed a crooked smile, full of pain, which faded instantly. "But I want to *do* something. I feel so helpless!"

"I'm sure the police are doing all they can," Mrs. Swann replied, trying to comfort – though the look Mark caught on Gary's face seemed to say "and that's precious little".

"Well, let's take your mind off things with a round or two of *Nemesis Pit*." Gary's face lit up as the idea came to him. He glanced at his sister. "Lee, will you make some of your famous banana milkshakes to bring up? We'll be in the bedroom."

"Will I be able to find you with all the mess in there?" she wondered, as the boys headed for the stairs.

☠

Mark had thought often that Gary was going to grow up to be a mad-professor type. The chaos in his bedroom only added to that impression. His bed was covered with games catalogs and computer magazines, and looked as though it hadn't been properly made for a week. Gary's desk similarly was littered with scraps of paper covered with scribbled notes, floppy disks tossed carelessly to one side, chocolate bar wrappers, and other junk. The screen showed a bottomless pit with colored stars spiraling into it. Every few seconds, a monstrous face loomed up and sank back down again into darkness.

"I got to level thirty-one last night," Gary said, as Mark pushed a pile of books off a spare chair and carried it to the desk, stepping carefully over the debris strewn all across the floor. But today he wasn't boasting, Mark realized, just trying to get him involved.

He watched as Gary's hands flickered across the keyboard. The creature from the Nemesis Pit, huge, green, dragonlike, rushed out at them, all teeth and fire. It roared and blew a blast of purple flame at the boys. Gary laughed and turned up the volume on his speakers to high. The monster snarled again, and this time Mark felt the vibrations in the floor under his feet. He chuckled.

"The trouble cleared up then?"

"Soon after we spoke on the phone. It faded as the thunderstorm died down – I guess the whole thing was caused by static in the air."

16

"Yeah, I suppose so." Mark glanced out through the window. The sky was very still this morning, overcast with gray-white clouds that had a metallic sheen as the sun shone through them: typical autumn weather, Mark thought – except it *felt* wrong. Deep down inside, he knew things were not normal…

Which was just plain ridiculous.

"I can set up a two-player game," Gary was saying, "or we can link up with some of the other gamers on the Net if you *really* want a fight on your hands!"

Leila came in with the milkshakes on a tray. She was grinning broadly and seemed very pleased with herself.

"Never mind that silly nonsense. I've been on the telephone, doing something useful – "

"Arranging plastic surgery maybe," Gary smirked. Leila poked her tongue out at him.

"Actually, no." She looked at Mark and handed him a shake. "Have you heard of a television show called 'Case on the Case'?"

"SBTV broadcasts it, don't they?"

"That's the one. It's Solid Broadcast's most popular show."

"I don't really watch it. Mom does, I think. It's about that detective guy – "

"Roy Case – and he really *is* a detective. He solves all kinds of mysteries and reconstructs them for episodes of his show."

Gary gave a huge mock-yawn and pretended to examine his fingernails. "Can we watch some paint dry, or something? That would be much more interesting."

Leila's eyes flashed. "Gary, I'm trying to help here." She turned back to Mark.

"Well, the thing is, I met Roy Case when our class went on a tour of the studios last term. I told him how I wanted to make wildlife documentaries as a career, and he said if I ever needed to ask any questions about TV work, he'd be happy to answer them."

"I bet he says that to all the girls who swoon at his feet!" Gary shook his head and tutted.

"He isn't like that at all. Well, he can't be, can he – because I've just called him and he says he wants to help trace Tina. We can meet him for lunch at the studio."

"It's only because it would make a good episode for his series – "

"So what!" Leila's temper flared at last. Mark realized that she, too, was upset by Tina's disappearance and felt as frustrated about it as he did.

Leila stepped over to Gary, kicking a pair of discarded running shoes out of her way. They went spinning across into the corner.

"So what if he is only doing it for himself? It's still help, isn't it? It's still help we need!"

Gary backed off, holding up his hands in surrender.

"You think it's a good idea, don't you, Mark?" Leila asked him.

"Um, of course," he said, though without much conviction, and adding mentally, "anything is better than nothing."

Chapter 4

The Solid Broadcast television studio was a twenty-story building close to the city center. A tall transmission tower added to its impressive height. On a clear night, Mark could see the lights on that tower flashing red from his bedroom window. It was one of Kenniston's most familiar landmarks.

Leila led the boys through a large, revolving glass door into a spacious lobby, where dozens of people seemed to be running around on urgent business.

"Don't you find this exciting?" Leila said. Gary blew out a great sigh.

"I just realized I forgot my Game Boy," he told her.

They introduced themselves at reception. A very fashionably dressed lady checked a list, then asked them to fill in their names and addresses on some cards.

"Thank you," she said as they handed them back. "Mr. Case asked me to direct you to the cafeteria. That's up on the ninth floor. Will you recognize him, or – "

"Oh," Leila said with a broad smile, "I'll recognize him all right!"

Gary pretended to push his fingers down his throat to make himself sick.

☠

The elevator ride was smooth and swift, delivering them to a large, airy dining room with a huge, panoramic window along one wall.

"There he is!" Leila pointed across the room to a table where a dark-haired man in his mid-thirties was sitting alone, staring out across the city. "Mr. Case – Mr. Case!"

Several people glanced up as Gary, blushing deeply, tried to hide behind Mark. "I hate this," he muttered, as Leila grabbed the boys' hands and dragged them toward where Roy Case was sitting.

He stood as they approached, grinning at their various reactions.

"Leila," Roy smiled. "Good to see you again." He shook her hand. "And, I see by the resemblance, this must be your brother – "

"I think you just insulted him," Leila quipped. "Yes, this is Gary, and Gary's friend, Mark Watkins."

Roy Case's face became serious. "So Tina is your sister?"

"Yes, sir. She's been missing since yesterday evening. If you can help, that'd be great."

"I'll do what I can, of course. And please, call me Roy. Now, sit yourselves down. I'll order some coffee and you can tell me all about it."

"…So you think MZTV might have something to do with it?" Leila said, twenty minutes later, once Mark had told his story. Roy had listened intently during this time, not looking particularly at any of the children, and not interrupting, but obviously taking everything in. Now, at Leila's question, he pushed his hand through his thick

20

black hair and leaned back in the seat.

"Impossible to say at this point, but it's a lead worth investigating – if only because MZTV is almost a complete mystery to just about everyone in the television business."

"I've never even heard of it," Gary admitted.

Roy shrugged. "You would have soon enough. A year ago, the company didn't exist, but it's been growing fast, gaining hundreds, maybe thousands of new viewers each week."

"The shows must be great," Mark said. Roy grimaced and shook his head.

"That's the strange thing – they're not. I've seen some of them, and they all appear to be really creaky old black and white movies, or ancient serials from so far back that none of the stars are even alive now! Why people pay to watch MZTV, I just don't know, but they do. And the studio is spending a fortune in advertising: posters, vouchers, free baseball caps and T-shirts and stuff. Maybe that has something to do with it."

"You say people pay to watch?" Mark asked. "Is it a satellite station?"

"No, it's entirely cable," Roy said. "That's another problem – if MZTV ever started to *broadcast* programs, there's a real risk other stations in Kenniston would be forced to close down. It's survival of the fittest in this business," he said, his smile wavering ever so slightly.

Shortly afterward, Roy took them on a tour of the studios, showing them where some of Solid Broadcast's programs were made. He introduced the children to Andy Hitchman, the head of SBTV, and finished off the tour with an elevator ride to the roof, where they could see the transmission tower up close.

"It's *huge*," Leila gasped, tilting her head back to glimpse the top.

"It adds another hundred feet to the height of the building," Roy said, "and transmits programs to over a million people, right across the city and far beyond."

Gary put his hands on his hips and gazed skyward.

"Wow, it's really impressive. I can't see MZTV ever putting you off the air."

"Television is a funny business," Roy said, as they started to walk back toward the elevator. He paused at the doorway and pointed at the mass of clouds to the north, where the heavens looked like a tangle of mangled, silver metal. The wind had strengthened in the past hour and, once again, the air smelled dry and tangy, as though full of lightning.

"It's happened before that small, unknown studios have grown large and powerful very quickly. And over there, on the horizon, is where the new threat is coming from. That's where the MZTV studios are to be found – just where the storm is gathering."

Chapter 5

"Well, is there anything he can do?" Sarah Watkins wanted to know, when Mark eventually came home. Her voice sounded flat and toneless, as though she had gone through the hurt and the worry, and all that was left was weariness.

"You've watched his show, Mom," Mark said, hating to see his mother looking so washed out. "Roy Case *always* solves the puzzle!"

Sarah smiled weakly. "But it's make-believe, Mark. It's just a television program."

"Based on real cases."

"Yes, I know, but only the ones he's managed to crack. What about all the cases he wasn't successful with? You never hear about those, do you?"

"No, but…," Mark began, and then stopped, knowing that to argue would be pointless. Instead, he walked over to her and gave her a big hug. Until a year or so ago, Sarah had been bigger than her son. Now the position was reverzed and he was taller, heavier, stronger. And Mark realized also that, with Tina gone, he was the one his mother would be looking to for comfort and support. To argue with her would be the worst thing he could possibly do.

As he held her, Sarah Watkins's body began to shake with silent sobbing. For a whole day she had been holding this in, all the panic and confusion, the terrible feeling that maybe she'd never see her daughter again. This was the first time she'd cried. Mark didn't try to stop her.

"Let it out, Mom, just let it out. Everything will be okay, I promise," he added, the lie slipping easily from his lips.

Sarah went to bed early, taking a pill to help her sleep. Mark recalled she hadn't done that since Dad had left, over four years ago. They'd managed fine, just the three of them, and Mark remembered thinking after the shock of his father's departure had cooled: so who needs him anyway?

We do, the thought flashed into his mind as he walked alone through the house, checking that doors and windows were properly locked. *We really need you now, Dad...*

Mark chuckled as he climbed the stairs to his room, telling himself that was a stupid thing to think. Paul Watkins had walked out on his family one night without any warning, leaving behind just a short, handwritten note explaining that he couldn't stand being tied down anymore, that he wanted to be free.

He'd never been in touch since that day.

☠

The screen saver on Mark's computer displayed an ever-changing collage of dinosaur heads, and every few seconds low growls and snuffling sounds came from the speakers mounted at the sides. The machine had been a combined Christmas and birthday present last year, though he'd had to save himself for the games he liked to play.

Seeing the familiar faces of T-Rex, Velociraptor, Stegosaurus, and others made Mark smile. He decided to play *Mutant Wars* again tonight, just for an hour or so, to take his mind off everything – and hoped he wouldn't be bothered by the ghostly faces he'd seen before. Probably just a freak effect of the weather, Mark mused, just like Gary had said.

He sat down at the desk, just as the phone rang in the hallway below.

Mark leaped up and hurried down the stairs. If it was news about Tina, then he'd wake Sarah and tell her; if it wasn't, he didn't want her to wake at all, not until late morning. She needed a good long rest.

He picked up the receiver.

"Mark – "

"Gary?" Mark felt pleased and disappointed at the same time. "What's up?"

"Roy Case phoned us. He's arranged for us all to go on a tour of the MZTV studios tomorrow morning, if you want to come."

"Well...I'm not sure I should leave Mom."

"Roy figures we should 'case the joint' – it's one of his little jokes. He's full of them. It would be good if you could come, Mark. What good are you doing just sitting around at home?"

"Well...," Mark said again, but he was convinced. Mrs. Dayne would probably be delighted to stop by again to keep Sarah company. Mrs. Dayne was one of the world's great gossips; she could talk nonstop the whole day, and would probably do so, too, given the opportunity.

Besides, if there was even the slightest chance that visiting MZTV could turn up a lead on Tina's whereabouts, it was worth doing.

"Okay, I'll come. What time, and where?"

"Nine a.m., outside Solid Broadcast. Roy says we can take a taxi across town. The tour starts at ten."

"I'll be there then."

"That's great. You having any more trouble with your computer?" Gary asked, as an afterthought.

"Nope. Back to normal. I was just about to run a game of *Mutant Wars*, just to beat the level you got to – thirty, wasn't it?"

"No, that was *Nemesis Pit*. I reached forty-two on 'Wars. Bad luck, Mark."

Mark could hear the mischievous laughter in his friend's voice as he wished Gary a good night and put down the phone. Forty-two, he thought, would be almost *impossible* to beat.

Back in his room, Mark switched on the lamp above his desk, flicked off the main light, and walked over to close the curtains. Through his window he could see the red caution lights flashing from SBTV's transmission tower across town. They were rather fuzzy and faint, because the night was misty and quite cool.

Close to the house, a streetlight shone through the bare branches of the lime tree in the yard and cast long, interwoven shadows across the large lawn. The Watkins's house stood on the corner of North Road and Patrick Street, and the garden formed a broad L-shape around it. To the left was the Dayne household, and beyond the rear fence lived Mr. and Mrs. Carpenter. They were an elderly couple who'd been married for centuries, it seemed to Mark, and spent most of their time watching TV.

This was what they were doing right now, Mark saw, noticing the flickering, silvery light of the television screen coming from a corner of their living room.

But then he looked again, more closely this time, frowning in concern as the TV light brightened suddenly, seeming to wash through the whole house. Then it faded just as quickly, leaving all the rooms in darkness.

Mark stared on into the gloom for long seconds afterward, wondering just what had happened. Perhaps there'd been an electrical short – maybe it had to do with the same kind of atmospheric interference that he and Gary had been plagued by.

But whatever it had been, Mark thought, it had looked very strange. Very strange indeed…

He left his room and returned to the telephone to call up the Carpenters and check to see if they were all right. Unlike Mrs. Dayne, the Carpenters didn't have much to do with any of their neighbors. They kept to themselves. Mark also remembered the times when one or the other of them had yelled at him for lobbing tennis balls over the fence and into their garden – really yelled, like they hated kids to bits. They weren't particularly nice people, in Mark's opinion. But even so, he wouldn't want to see them hurt.

He dialed the number and heard the rapid beeping of connections being made. Then there was only static, swishing and crashing far away like the shoreline of a distant sea. Mark sighed, realizing he'd need to go there in person.

Leaving the house quietly, he trotted down the driveway, turned left at the end, and left again onto Patrick Street. He went through the front gate to the Carpenters' house, slowing as he approached the front door, then rang the bell.

He heard it sound deep in the house, but nobody came. He pressed the button again, and a third time – shivering now in the night chill, as the wind stirred and twirled around him beneath the shadowy porch roof.

Part of Mark's mind told him that the best thing to do was go home and play *Mutant Wars* like he wanted. But another inner voice was persuading him to take a look around, because something was obviously wrong here.

He sighed and walked to the side of the house to peer through the living room window, where the curtains had been opened.

They were still there, allowing him to glimpse Mrs. Carpenter slumped in an easy chair, gazing with glassy, empty eyes at some old black and white movie playing on the television. Mark thought it looked really boring, but the old lady was obviously enjoying it, because her mouth was hanging open and amazingly she didn't blink once.

He shrugged, and was about to turn away when a figure rose up in the room, pressed its hands against the glass and glared at him.

"It's okay, Mr. Carpenter," Mark began, "it's only…"

But the words died in his throat.

The old man's eyes were flaring with blizzards of glowing particles. He opened his mouth and said something to Mark – but all he heard was the hissing of a dead TV channel, as he stumbled backward away from the window, wonder and terror rising through him like a wave.

Chapter 6

"Yeah, yeah, yeah," Gary said, as though Mark had told him he'd been kidnapped by aliens from outer space, "and on the way home you were attacked by a gang of Reptiloids from the Twilight Zone!"

It was the next morning. Mark, Gary, and Leila were standing in the bustling lobby of the Solid Broadcast building, waiting for Roy Case. To begin with, Mark had been reluctant to tell his friends about what he'd seen the night before – precisely because he knew that Gary would react this way.

"I know it sounds crazy, but – "

"Crazy!" Gary gave a hoot of laughter. Several people nearby turned to stare at the group. "I think you've been reading too many comic books."

"You're a fine one to talk," Leila chipped in, pushing her brother playfully on the arm. "You spend more time with your head in the clouds than anyone else I know."

Mark smiled at the girl's unexpected support. She looked at him, smiled back; and Mark blushed deeply, though he didn't quite know why.

"But it does sound *so* strange," Leila went on. "Maybe you did imagine it, Mark. You have been through a lot lately."

"Well…" It would have been easy to insist on what he'd seen, but Leila did have a point. Perhaps the strain of Tina's disappearance was telling on him. Perhaps he had imagined Mr. Carpenter's weird condition after all.

He shrugged and said no more about it, as Roy Case came hurrying out of the elevator toward them.

"Sorry guys, sorry…" He sounded out of breath. "Andy's been hitting the roof up in the Control Room - but I'll tell you about it on the way to MZTV. Come on, we're running late."

☠

"Static electrical discharges," Roy said doubtfully. "That's what the technical crew say it is. I'm not so sure. When systems crash and computers go haywire for no obvious reason, I'm tempted to think somebody's trying to *make* it happen."

They were in a taxi, heading downtown. At first their progress had been slow due to heavy rush hour traffic. But this had thinned out as they left Kenniston center behind. Now they were moving at a good speed through the industrial quarter, a sprawl of long, straight streets of factories, warehouses, and rail road yards.

"Industrial espionage?" Gary wondered, his eyes suddenly sparkling with excitement. Leila tutted at such a silly idea. Roy's expression was veiled.

"Could be. It's not impossible that a rival station might want to put us off the air – or even steal our ideas for upcoming programs. Anyway, what happened early this morning was enough to put Andy Hitchman in a panic."

"You say the studio's computer screens went fuzzy, and you could see faint images on them?" Mark asked. "Figures…faces?"

Roy nodded. "As though, by some freak of nature, a TV channel were breaking through into the network. But don't ask me how it could happen: the computer system is linked to the telephone network, not a television cable network."

"MZTV?" Leila wondered, lifting her eyebrows in query.

"That," said Roy, "among other things, is what I hope to find out today."

Ten minutes later, the cab turned a corner into a wide, run-down street which, Mark noticed from a nameplate, was called Hob's Lane. It was a gloomy place, made gloomier by the dingy façades of abandoned warehouses, their windows boarded up, their doors locked and bolted. The far end of Hob's Lane was cloaked in gray, morning mist.

The thickset driver slowed his vehicle, half turning to talk to Roy.

"You sure this is the place, pal?"

"It's a definite possibility," Roy answered, giving a rather nervous chuckle. "Keep going. Maybe it's at the other end of the street."

They cruised past half-ruined buildings and empty lots, some of them reduced to ugly landscapes of rubble, others nothing more than flat, weed-choked expanses of concrete or earth. High, chainlink fences or panels of rusting metal separated these wastelands from the street. Mark was reminded of the war-torn scenery from *Mutant Wars*, half expecting to see a Reptiloid Attack Squad appear over a nearby mound of bricks and twisted girders.

He was about to mention the idea, when Gary's breathless exclamation cut him short.

"Well, will you take a look at that!"

They all stared ahead, and Mark heard Leila gasp as a glittering tower of glass and steel loomed out of the mist ahead of them, its topmost floors blazing in the light of the morning sun.

"I don't think I quite believe it," Leila said in a small, subdued voice. "It's so new – so clean – amid all this dirt and wreckage."

The cab pulled up at the opposite curb. Several tourist buses had parked a little farther down the street. Streams of people were making their way toward the large front entrance – above which a sign in gleaming chrome lettering said:

MAX ZOFFANY TELEVISION

"It's sure an eye-opener," the taxi driver commented. "I don't come down here often; no need, you understand. But I'm positive the last time I drove by, maybe six months ago, this place didn't even exist!"

"Max Zoffany...MZTV." Mark shook his head in puzzlement. "Why would he build his studios in the middle of nowhere like this? It's miles from the city center."

"Cheap ground rent," Gary suggested. "Or maybe he wanted to help the local community."

Roy Case gave a slightly sarcastic laugh. He paid the driver and then led the children across the road and through the shining doorway into the studio.

☠

If possible, the interior was even more imposing than the outside of the building had been. Huge sculptures of polished steel, like soaring blades, swept upward from the floor at the far end of the huge vestibule. Hanging above them, supported by invisible threads, was a vast winged object, all angles and glowing metal surfaces.

"It's a bird," Leila judged, having looked at it hard. "And these blades are – "

"Flames!" Gary broke in. He pointed to the plush blue carpet stretching away into the distance. It was patterned with repeated shapes of a bird spreading its wings as it rose from a nest of fire. "It's a phoenix. According to legend, when the phoenix reaches the end of its life, it makes a funeral pyre and burns its old body away – then it rises, strong and vigorous again, from the ashes of its corpse."

"Well, I guess Max Zoffany did just that," Roy said, "creating this incredible place from a ruin. I'm impressed. Come on, it looks like the tour's about to begin."

A group of visitors had gathered around a table at which two MZTV tour guides, a man and a woman, were standing. Mark pointed to the freebie goodie bags being given out. People were delving into them and pulling out baseball caps,

T-shirts, photographs, stickers, even personal stereos – all finished in dark blue with the silver MZTV phoenix logo.

"Let's grab a couple!" Gary said, as he and Mark hurried forward through the crowd. But Leila hung back with Roy, her face shrouded in puzzlement.

"Have you noticed those tour guides?" she wondered. Roy nodded slowly.

"Both young, both very attractive…polite, friendly, cheerful…"

"Almost too good to be true." Leila gave a little sniff of disdain. "But not only that, Roy: look closely at them – they're both plastered in stage makeup, like they were actors playing a role. It's so thick you could scrape it off with your fingernails."

Roy chuckled as Leila gave a shudder. "They're just putting on a show for the crowd," he suggested. "Though you're right, it is a bit overdone. There's no need for quite so much makeup. It makes them look artificial," Roy added, half to himself, as Mark and Gary returned. "Almost brand new, straight out of the factory."

The four kept up with the group for a short time after the tour began. The pretty female guide led the visitors away from the imposing vestibule and through sparkling new corridors, past offices where smart, young personnel were busy at their desks, working on computers and speaking into telephones. Shortly afterward they passed a small studio where an advertisement for Max Zoffany's television station was being filmed.

"We hope to get this broadcast through other local channels," the guide explained brightly, "to attract even more viewers to MZTV."

"Do you suppose other television companies will run your ad?" Roy asked. "I mean, if you become too popular, you'll put some of the smaller stations out of business."

"Oh, we don't mind if other stations advertise with us. It's fair competition." The girl lightly shrugged her shoulders, as though the issue were settled.

"It must be very expensive to run television commercials," Roy continued, as the girl was about to turn away. "Max Zoffany must have plenty of money behind him?"

"Mr. Zoffany – " The girl's face clouded and her eyes became distant, as though she were looking at something far away or deep inside her mind. People in the crowd glanced at one another unsurely.

Then her face shone in a beaming smile.

"Mr. Zoffany knows exactly what he's doing. Don't worry, our campaign will be successful. Soon MZTV will be the most popular station in the city…in the world. And now, if you'll follow me, ladies and gentlemen, we can resume the tour…"

"That," commented Gary a few minutes later, "was *weird*. It was like she was listening to instructions from somewhere – but I didn't see an earpiece or anything."

"As you say," Roy agreed, nodding, "weird. And frustrating, too. She's not taking us anywhere near the heart of the station. We haven't seen the

36

control room, the editing suite, the sound studio…It's as though we're just scratching the surface: being shown carefully chosen fragments of something much greater."

"Do you, um, suppose we could look for Tina?" Mark asked hesitantly.

Roy's eyes showed sympathy. He rested his hand on Mark's shoulder as he said: "The time isn't right yet, son. We have very little to go on – and no evidence at all that anyone here was involved in Tina's disappearance. Before we do anything else, we need to gather that evidence, find the clues that will lead us quickly to her."

The tour had moved on as Roy explained this, turning a corner at the far end of the corridor. The guide's singsong voice faded into the distance as Roy and the children found themselves alone.

"Perhaps," he said, smiling mischievously, "we might search for a couple of those clues right now…"

They backtracked along the corridor until they came to a door that the tour had bypassed. Roy glanced at the kids with eyebrows raised.

"It's as good as any," Leila said, pushing it open and striding determinedly through.

Instantly she found herself wrapped in clinging fog, which surged around her in a chilling gust of wind. Cold rain began to fall from the dismal sky. Lightning flared once, dazzling.

The shock made Leila stumble forward. Roy grabbed her to prevent her from falling. "We're outside!" she said, aghast. "The door leads nowhere!" She was gasping with the shock of the freezing wind and her unexpected surroundings. "And the weather's closed in!"

"It's in back of the studios." Gary swept his hand to indicate the wide expanse of wasteland, a desolation of churned soil and piles of rubble. "How come?"

Thunder tumbled across the sky in the lightning's wake. The rain began coming down more heavily.

"Let's get inside." Roy hustled the others back through the door. "Um, maybe we should rejoin the tour now. I'll check the place out myself later."

Despite the children's protests, Roy insisted, and would offer no explanation for his decision.

But they had not seen the security guard patroling near the boundary fence, Roy thought. The man's face looked bone-white and half melted by the rain…

Nor had they noticed the dog walking beside him. A huge beast, wolf-sized, with the reddest, deadliest eyes that Roy had ever seen.

Chapter 7

Roy said nothing of what he'd seen on the journey back across town. It was not that he wasn't sure: there was no doubt in his mind that there, in the empty back lot of MZTV, he had spotted a man that appeared more dead than alive, and a dog that might have sprung straight out of a horror movie. Nor was he worried that the kids might disbelieve him. He didn't care one way or the other about that.

What concerned Roy most – and what frightened him again as he thought back to it – was the look of evil in the eyes of both the guard and his animal. A look that was barely human. A dark, sinister, *dangerous* look.

It was not something that he wanted Leila, Mark, or Gary involved with. Much better, Roy thought, if they stayed right out of it while he completed his investigation into Tina's disappearance. Maybe the Zoffany Studios were connected, or perhaps not. Roy hoped not, because if he had to return there even once more, that would be once too often as far as he was concerned.

Roy directed the taxi driver to drop Leila and Gary off first. "I'll call you when I have some news," he promised, smiling rather thinly as the car pulled away. He wound up the window and avoided looking at Mark's face.

Mark made no mention of it until they were halfway home. By then, he couldn't stand the silence any longer.

"What's wrong?" he asked, adding, before Roy could deny it, "I know something is, so why don't you tell me?"

Roy tried to bluff his way through by suggesting he had a pile of other work he needed to catch up on: phone calls to make, meetings with Andy Hitchman about a possible new series of "Case on the Case", people to interview… But Mark knew that was all a pretense for his benefit. Something had happened back at MZTV that Roy wanted to hide. And if he was not willing to reveal what it was, then, Mark reasoned, it had to have something to do with Tina…

They arrived at Mark's home a few minutes later. Sarah Watkins was already waiting for them on the front porch.

"Gary's mom must have phoned ahead." Mark grinned rather sheepishly. "My mother and Mrs. Swann rank among the world's greatest gossips. She'll know all about what's happened today. And she's bound to invite you in for coffee – and, if you're really unlucky, she'll offer you a slice of her homemade fruitcake, too. Sorry."

Roy laughed at the boy's embarrassment. The cab pulled up and Roy pushed open the door for Mark to step out. He followed.

Sarah was eager to greet them, Mark thought, as he led Roy up the driveway toward the house. "It's a miracle she hasn't gotten her autograph book out already," he added.

40

"Don't feel bad about it – TV people like me need fans as much as we need fresh air."

He smiled broadly and shook Sarah Watkins's outstretched hand. "Won't you come in for coffee?" she invited. "I'd love to hear what you've been up to today. Oh, and I have some fruit cake, freshly made. I'll bet you're half starved…"

Mark groaned softly as his mother ushered Roy into the house.

☠

It pleased Mark that Roy didn't lift Sarah's hopes falsely. He explained that, until he could uncover *how* Tina had vanished and *why*, there would be little chance of retracing her movements since then.

"People disappear for all kinds of reasons, Mrs. Watkins – and before you say 'But that's not like Tina' – well, it's what every parent says when their children don't come home."

"Do you think she could have been – kidnapped?"

Sarah's smile had faded as Roy spoke. Now it was gone entirely and the sparkle of tears was back in her eyes. Roy glanced at Mark before answering.

"That's one possibility, sure. But there are many others. Look, I'll be honest with you. Mark and Leila and Gary have asked me to investigate this case, and I'm happy to do that to the best of my ability. I have contacts among the police, and in plenty of other places, believe me. I can work fast, and I often get results. But I can't offer any guarantees – no one can do that, Mrs. Watkins, no one at all."

"I appreciate your frankness, Mr. Case." She struggled to control her anguish.

"And I know that you're doing all you can to help find Tina. But it's so hard, just waiting…"

"Sure it is, but I'll keep you up to date. And please," he added, "call me Roy."

"Well – " She gave a half-hearted smile, "I will if you call me Sarah."

Mark felt a strange anger rushing up through his body as Roy and his mother talked. He put his coffee mug heavily down on the table, so both of them looked at him.

"Since you're being so honest, Roy," Mark said, ignoring Sarah's disapproving glare, "maybe you'd explain to Mom what scared you at MZTV."

"I don't know what – "

"You've been trying to hide it since we left the studio. What's going on there that you're not telling us?"

"Mark, don't speak to Roy like that!"

"Tell me – come on, Mr. Detective, *tell me!*"

"That's enough, Mark!" Sarah Watkins rose from her seat and started to move forward. Roy leaned out and clasped her forearm.

"Sarah, it's okay. The boy's been through a lot, just as you have." He turned to Mark. "If I knew that something was 'going on' at MZTV, I'd tell you both. But I don't deal in maybe's. I hope you'll accept that, son."

"I won't accept it. You're lying to us – *you're lying to us!*"

Mark stood up and ran to the door, feeling suddenly very foolish as well as angry and confused. He turned as he reached it and said, quietly but forcefully, "And don't you ever call me your son…"

He slammed the door behind him as he hurried to his room.

☠

Mark lay on his bed for a long time, listening to the quiet, steady voices rising up through the floorboards from the living room below. He could not make out what Roy and his mother were saying, but he was able to judge their tone. Roy was calm and reassuring; Sarah grateful and so obviously relieved that now she didn't have to carry the burden of Tina's absence alone. Somebody was standing by her…

And that somebody, Mark thought bleakly, isn't me any longer.

A few minutes later the tone of the adults' voices changed. The living room door clicked as it was opened.

Mark swung himself off his bed and walked to the small guest bedroom at the front of the house, which overlooked the driveway.

Roy was telling Sarah that he'd hail a cab as soon as he reached the main road. He insisted again that she shouldn't worry – and that maybe it would be best if he worked on the case alone, from now on. "Kids slow me down," he said lightly.

"So you don't think the people at the studios

would know anything?" Sarah wondered.

"No, I think that's a false trail. But I'll go down that way tomorrow and ask around. You never know what might turn up."

Mark felt his fists clenching as Roy and his mother said their goodnights. He had no idea why Roy should be hiding something from him - but he knew that he was.

And Mark also knew exactly what he was going to do about it.

Chapter 8

Roy Case stared at the TV screen in his apartment without really seeing it. He was deep in thought, mulling over all that had happened that day. He found himself going through his first meeting with Sarah Watkins. Mark's attitude concerned him, but Roy understood it and forgave him. He realized that Mark had been the man of the house since his father had walked out, and perhaps now he saw Roy as an intruder, even a rival for Sarah's affections.

A warm, slow smile spread across Roy's face. Affections? He was probably reading far too much into the situation. Sure, Sarah was a very attractive lady, and seemed not to dislike Roy, if first impressions were to be trusted. But it would be foolish to believe that a chance meeting, a polite exchange of conversation, could develop into something more. Though if it did, Roy knew he would not stop it from happening. Because here he was: wealthy, famous, envied – and very lonely.

The smile faded and Roy absently reached for the mug on the table at his side. Now he was thinking about MZTV; not just his glimpse of the security guard and his monstrous dog, but other, smaller things that chewed at his mind… The way the tour guides had been plastered with makeup – "Too good to be true," as Leila had said – and the way the building itself had appeared almost magically out of the wasteland during the past few months. The shining steel and glass also seemed too good to be true. And why had Zoffany built his studios there, right out of town, amid the wreckage and rubble of the past? And who was Max Zoffany anyway? Roy had checked with Andy and some of his other TV friends, and nobody – *nobody* – had ever heard of the man.

"Questions, questions, questions…," Roy whispered to himself as he finished his drink and glanced at his watch. Plenty of questions, but no answers yet. And what had started out as a simple case of tracking down a missing girl was turning into a much deeper, much darker mystery.

It was 9:30 in the evening. Roy knew that the only way to pick up some leads was to return to the Zoffany studios and look around on his own terms. He figured that the building would be largely deserted by now, with perhaps just a small night staff on duty, and one or maybe two security men. He'd snuck into places plenty of times before, but realized he was hesitating on this particular occasion.

On an impulse, Roy stood up and strode into the hallway for his jacket and car keys. He snatched them off the hall table and stood for a second, his attention caught by the reflection of his own face in the mirror, a face that showed determination and confidence, to be sure, but also a surprising depth of fear.

☠

He parked two blocks from the studios and walked the rest of the way to Hob's Lane. The streets were deserted, as Roy had expected them to be. A few ancient streetlights cast sparse, dismal circles of amber light along the pavement. At the far end of the block, the MZTV building stood like a great, glass headstone in the dead wilderness, its many windows glinting in the upward-slanting beams of a single powerful spotlight.

Roy kept to the shadows, which was easy to do as he made his way quickly and silently to the gate in the chainlink fence that bordered Zoffany's land. Upon reaching the gate, he saw the padlock lying at his feet: it had been sawed cleanly through. He picked it up and hefted its weight in his hand while he considered his options.

It looked as though someone had broken in earlier; but who, and why? Either that, or this was a clever trap, perhaps set for Roy himself. Maybe he'd been recognized on the tour as the famous TV detective, and Zoffany anticipated his return. If that was true, then Zoffany certainly had something to hide.

Roy placed the padlock back on the ground and eased himself through the metal gateway. His eyes, by now, had adjusted to the darkness. He could make out the jagged hills of old brickwork, the rusted iron girders thrusting up from the soil like the skeletal remains of some vast prehistoric beast, tangles of wire and scattered spars of wood – all that now remained of whatever had stood here in the past. No light was showing from any of the windows in the studio building, so maybe, Roy thought, he was in luck.

His plan was to enter by the doorway Leila had

stumbled through earlier. That would lead him right to the heart of the studio. Roy squinted as he picked his way carefully over the broken ground – then fell back with a cry, as a dark shape rose up in front of him and grabbed ahold of his jacket.

For a few dreadful seconds, all of Roy's childhood nightmares surged back through his mind: those early fears of the dark and the monsters it contained. His arms flailed out as he struggled to dislodge the clinging thing from his body.

Then cool reason flooded through him. He stopped struggling, realizing that whoever this person was, he was terrified, much more frightened than Roy was.

"Hey, take it easy. It's okay, it's – "

The person looked up at him and Roy's eyes widened.

"Mark!" he said, in utter shock. "What the hell are you doing here?"

☠

Crouched down behind a mound of rubble, Roy listened as Mark told his story. After Roy had left the house, Mark had disbelieved his promise to help. "I guessed you thought the case wasn't important enough to investigate," Mark said with a trembling smile. "You said there were no leads here at MZTV – but I knew there must be, so I decided to search the studio myself. I cut through the lock with a hacksaw and started to head for the building. But then – I saw – "

"What did you see?" Roy asked gently. The boy wiped at his eyes roughly with the back of his hand. Roy reached out and clasped his shoulders.

"It's okay to be afraid, Mark…This place is enough to spook anyone. It sure spooks me!"

Mark chuckled at the tone of the man's voice. Roy went on. "You did a brave thing, you know – no really," he added, as Mark shook his head. "Courage is doing what you fear to do, and it scared you to come here – "

"I had to. This is where Tina disappeared, I *know* it is!"

"We don't know, not yet," Roy said softly. "But since we both have our suspicions, and since we both turned up tonight – maybe we'd better work together in finding some answers. What do you say?"

Mark stared hard at the man's face, searching for sincerity and finding it there. He nodded, holding out his hand for Roy to grasp in a firm grip of friendship.

"Now," Roy said, "tell me what you saw."

"It was over there." Mark pointed beyond the rubble heap. "Maybe I'd better show you."

They made their way around the heap to a place where the ground dipped, sloping away toward the studio building. Roy glanced at the hollow, then looked around uneasily. The night was absolutely still, the sky a gloomy overhang of cloud, faintly underlit by the distant glow of the city center.

"Something was moving in the earth," Mark said simply, his voice flat. "I saw it – something huge making the soil heave upward…"

Roy opened his mouth to challenge it – but no words came from his suddenly tightening throat.

The ground *was* moving, just as Mark had said. The whole crater floor seemed to be rippling, lifting upward into a vast dome of dirt and rocks.

Then the dome split into a hail of small stones and fragments, and from out of it rose huge black girders that surged closer and locked together in a clanging cacophony of sound, like the work of invisible giants. Hundreds of bricks followed after, each one glowing a dull red, as though fresh from the kiln. They flung themselves at the towering structure of metal, miraculously tumbling into place to form bare walls. Then unbroken sheets of glass slid from the soil and flew upward, spinning in the night, fitting neatly into the newly created window spaces. Finally, showers of rivets, nails, trims, scraps, and fragments swept into the air and whirled around the edifice, rattling and tinkling on the metal and brick and glass until each one could slot perfectly into place.

Both Roy and Mark had hunched down instinctively to avoid being hit, and had so far escaped harm. But now, out of the ground, burst a geyser of intense blue flame that sprayed against the framework, licking it over with fire.

In seconds the heat became unbearable.

Mark shrieked in pain. Roy grabbed his arm and began dragging him away. If only they could make it to shelter nearby. But the boy was dead weight, too shocked to run.

"Come on, help yourself, Mark!" Roy yelled. "We just need to – "

Something slammed into the side of his head, sending him sprawling to the ground.

The world spun and tumbled, and bright, wet stars exploded across Roy's vision. He tried to focus, tried to stand…but a leather-gloved hand pushed him back.

"Mark!" he shouted, fearing for the boy's safety.

The security guard's face loomed into view. Dull white bone was visible where the parchment skin had dried and dropped away. The thing had no ears at all, and no lips: its smile was fixed and skull-like.

But most remarkable of all were the creature's eyes, flashing and flaring like crazy TV screens, as the guard bore down for the kill.

Chapter 9

Roy punched upward without thinking, his fingers crunching on hard bone. The skeleton-man was momentarily stunned but seemed to feel no pain, and an instant later began forcing its head closer to Roy's face, its mouth opening wide.

Roy let out a grunt of desperation and sheer effort as, instead of trying to force the creature away, he pulled it closer – bringing his legs up under his opponent's stomach, rolling backward to pitch the attacker over his head.

The security guard sailed through the air for several yards and came to land in a sprawl of stick like limbs among a pile of broken bricks. It struggled feebly, attempting vainly to right itself and continue the fight.

Roy rolled lightly and came up on his feet, crouched and ready to face another assault; but the eyes of the skeleton-thing were fading, as though its energy were drained. It was beaten.

Roy turned and searched for Mark in the darkness, not spotting him at once because the boy was standing absolutely still, his eyes fixed on two blood-red pinpoints glowing from the top of a rubble heap.

And behind the points of light came a low, menacing snarl.

"Mark – " Roy said in a harsh whisper. "Don't move!" Then he realized what a stupid comment that was: obviously the kid was too terrified to move – or sensible enough to realize that, if he did, the savage guard dog would attack.

Slowly, gradually, Roy bent at the knees and eased himself down, never taking his eyes from those terrible, glaring lights as he searched for a weapon: a rock, a length of metal, even a piece of wood – anything that might possibly be of use against this monster.

The rumbling growl came again, followed by a tiny clattering of stones from the top of the pile.

Oh my God, Roy thought, *it's ready to pounce!*

His fingers found a brick half buried in the earth. He grasped and pulled, and felt it loosen like a tooth drawn from a rotten jaw.

The dog's blazing eyes shifted and its growling rose in pitch.

Roy stood upright, drew back his arm, and hurled the brick through the air as the creature suddenly sprang. He heard the dull thud of it striking the animal's body, the angry snarling becoming a shrill yelp of pain.

Then he was blinded. A swathe of light cut through the night and illuminated the gigantic dog in full flight. It was vast, maybe twice the size of the largest Doberman Roy had ever encountered; its almost-hairless skull and body was grayish, the color of old lead. Its crushing jaws were packed with razor teeth.

Roy registered this in a split-second, before the beast twisted, arching back in agony, its body all at once erupting into a ball of yellow flame that faded swiftly to leave a spiraling swirl of shadows and a few scraps of charred skin, which drifted away on the breeze.

Mark swung his torch toward Roy and dazzled him all over again.

"Wow!" he breathed, "it's just like the Power Scimitar in *Mutant Wars*!"

Roy gave a great, shuddering sigh of relief. He walked over to Mark and ruffled his hair.

"Whatever it's like, it saved our lives." He glanced over at the motionless security guard, and then at a paper-thin fragment of the dog's burned remains: its edges were glowing with sparks, slowly fading.

"They're creatures of the night, Mark. Light must be deadly to them."

"We must remember that the next time we come here…"

"Now wait just one minute, young man – " Roy began. Mark jiggled the flashlight and smiled.

"Uh-uh, Roy. You said yourself that we should work together to find some answers. Well, I figure all we've done is bring up a whole new pile of questions. Besides, with enemies like *those*, I think you need all the help you can get!"

"I can't argue with that," Roy agreed, chuckling. "And you're right, of course; we do need to check out MZTV more thoroughly - but in the daylight. For now, I think I ought to get you home."

They hurried as quickly as they could back toward the boundary fence, then along the streets to where Roy's car was parked. Roy revved up the engine, flicked on the headlights, and started to drive away.

"Oh – my bike," Mark remembered as the car built up speed. He pointed out through the windshield. "I left it up here at the end of the street."

Roy made a small expression of annoyance, but slowed anyway as he caught sight of the bicycle. "Okay, you pick it up. The trunk's unlocked."

Mark clambered out of the car and hurried around to the rear. He lifted open the trunk lid and turned to retrieve the bike.

Roy spotted the black dog in the same instant, moving swiftly and silently toward them. It was just as large as the one they'd destroyed in the wasteland: as large, and equally deadly. With a cunning that Roy found hard to believe, the creature was carefully avoiding the cones of yellow streetlights, and the car's bright headlight beams. Its awful jaws hung agape in a savage grin.

"Get in the car!" Roy yelled out, realizing Mark had left his flashlight on the dashboard. He fumbled desperately with the gearshift, intending to maneuver the car to catch the dog in the beams. The gearbox crunched and whined; the car lurched and stalled.

Roy swore and twisted the ignition key in a panic. There was a loud clatter as Mark threw his bike in the trunk. Then the boy slid back down into the passenger seat, breathless and trembling.

The black dog leaped from ten yards away and crashed into the windshield.

Mark flung his hands in front of his face, but Roy resisted the impulse. He forced a calming breath, turned the key more slowly, and slipped the gearshift into first.

The windshield was made of toughened glass. It fractured and bowed inward, but didn't shatter.

The engine bellowed, high-revving. Roy floored the accelerator pedal and the car jerked forward, tires spinning on the slick asphalt, smoke spiraling up.

Then the wheels found their grip and the car moved quickly away. Mark heard the squeal and slither of great claws scrabbling along the roof. Roy wrenched at the steering wheel; the car's back end tilted sideways and the beast slid away, tumbling into the road.

Mark twisted himself around to see it. The thing rolled in a flail of legs, then righted itself and stood looking after the speeding car, not bothering to give chase. Maybe it can't, he thought: maybe it must stay close to the wasteland.

Its terrible blood-lit eyes vanished as it turned away into the night.

"Mark." Roy's voice broke into the boy's thoughts. "Help me push out this windshield. Can't see a damned thing."

Mark leaned forward and thumped at the sheet of flexing glass with the flats of his hands. Roy helped with his left hand. The whole windshield popped outward after a few moments, the panel slipping down and to the left over the car's nearest fender.

The cold night chill poured in as Roy reached the end of the street and swung the car around the corner – into the path of a second security guard, as decayed and menacing as the first.

Unlike the black dog, the guard was unaffected by the headlight beams. He was carrying two long spars of metal, one of which he now hefted like a spear and hurled with great accuracy at the car, bearing down.

Roy jerked his head aside. The iron pole whispered past, missing him by an inch, drilling cleanly through the rear windshield to clang into the roadway behind.

"Keep your head low," Roy advised, but Mark's full attention was fixed on the guard, on that frightening skeleton grin, the gleaming fingerbones, the fizzing silver lightning where its eyes ought to have been.

The guard raised the second spar into position.

Roy dropped down a gear and stamped hard on the throttle. The car hit the creature at sixty with a bang. The thing exploded into a whirl of dust and rotting cloth and spinning ribs – except for the head, which bounced up along the hood and into the car.

It landed between Mark and Roy. And Mark gave a groan of disgust to see that the head was still active, the eyes blazing yet, the mouth snapping open and shut as the thing tried to sink its teeth into the flesh of Roy's leg.

The car was swerving this way and that across the road as Roy tried to wipe dust and particles out of his eyes.

The head rolled to the side against his leg.

With a grimace of pure revulsion, Mark wound down the passenger window, leaned over to pick

up the head by its lank, cobwebby hair, and flung
it out into the darkness.

Chapter 10

"That," Mark said, looking at the familiar frontage of his own home, "is something I never want to go through again." He glanced up at Roy.

The man gave a wry chuckle, which faded as he saw that shock and fear were still bright in Mark's eyes. "Well, the nightmare is not over yet – in fact, it's barely begun." He shrugged. "But we're still no closer to finding Tina, and it may be that MZTV isn't even connected with her disappearance."

"But you don't believe that," Mark said. It was not a question.

"No," Roy answered after a pause. "I don't believe that at all."

"So I'll have to go through it again. And maybe much worse, before she's found."

"Only if you want to."

Mark gave a fragile smile. " 'Courage is doing what you fear to do.' "

"But it also takes courage to put your trust in a stranger, as you're doing with me. No one will call you a coward if you choose to back out now."

Mark looked away from Roy, along the quiet avenue with its autumn-browned trees and veils of mist hanging motionlessly under the streetlights. It all seemed so peaceful, the danger so far away…

But then he recalled the odd glinting light in Mr. Carpenter's eyes, and realized that the evil might have crept much nearer to home than Roy or he had suspected.

"I'm not going to back out," Mark said with a

quiet determination. "Not until this is over with."

Roy grinned – perhaps with relief, Mark wondered – and the two shook hands.

"Okay, that's great, Mark. But look, keep things to yourself for now. Your mom needn't know what's happened; she shouldn't be more upset than she already is. And it might be wise if you didn't even tell Gary and Leila. The more people who know, the more likely Zoffany is to hear about it and realize we're on to him."

"I'll do my best," Mark agreed. "But it sure is a hard secret to keep to yourself!"

Roy nodded. "It's a problem, I know - but not as great as the one I've got."

Mark frowned. "What's that?"

"Trying to work out what to say to my insurance company when I put in a claim for this car!"

☠

Roy found he could not use his regular parking space outside the apartment block where he lived. During the evening, workmen had evidently been busy digging a trench for some purpose unknown to him. The work was still not complete: a barrier of red and white wooden stands bordered the trench, beyond which a long mound of dirt still lay. Gas mains perhaps, Roy thought, or the water company repairing a leaking pipe.

He sighed wearily, reversed his car away and parked elsewhere, laughing out loud as he activated the alarm, realizing he had no windshield in place. He tried to remember if he had a beer left in the fridge as he walked toward the front entrance to the building – failing to see the sinister, glowing silver light that rose from the trench once his back was turned.

☠

Sarah Watkins said nothing, which led Mark to believe she knew he'd been out of the house the night before. Today she looked tired, the skin around her eyes a little taut, but seeming brighter than she had been. Mark ran a bath for her, and while she enjoyed it he cooked breakfast and put coffee on to percolate.

She came into the kitchen in her blue bathrobe, her long, fair hair mussed up from toweling. Mark felt a little shock tear through his heart for an instant as he realized how much like Tina she looked. Just for that second, it might have *been* his sister, coming down for breakfast as though nothing were wrong at all.

Mark turned away to lift Sarah's breakfast plate from under the grill.

"Do you want help with the shopping?" he offered. "There's nothing left in the fridge."

He heard the rustle of the bathrobe, and then his mother's arms were hugging him, her face pressed close into his shoulder.

"I'm sorry, Mark," she whispered. "It must be so hard for you. I've spent all my time thinking about Tina and given no thought to your feelings. I don't know what I would do if you weren't here…"

Mark turned and put his arm around Sarah's shoulder and squeezed her, a little roughly because he felt embarrassed now by his mother's open show of feelings. He also felt what, perhaps, was anger, because Sarah seemed to be suggesting that Mark might walk out like his father had done.

"Let me pour you some coffee," he said, making it sound like an order. "And eat your eggs and bacon before they get cold."

☠

They went out shopping shortly afterward. Sarah owned a little red two-door hatchback, which she had bought at a used car lot four years earlier. It was the first big expense they'd been faced with, but a necessary one since Paul Watkins had taken the family car.

It was over a mile to the mall. Normally Sarah might have walked, but as Mark had rightly said, the fridge was empty and the normal business of life – eating regular meals, getting enough sleep – still had to go on. So the plan was to stock up the kitchen with enough food to last for a month.

They parked the car, took a cart from a long line of them near the store, and pushed it around to the supermarket's main entrance. They were greeted with what looked like a festival in full swing as they turned the corner.

Mark's jaw muscles clenched at the sight, and Sarah's face went pale.

A platform had been set up in the middle of

the mall, surmounted by a tentlike canopy, and above that a majestic blue banner. Emblazoned on the banner was the phoenix symbol of MZTV, rising from a bed of silver flames.

A hundred people or more were clustered around the publicity stand. Six or seven MZTV personnel were busily giving out the goodie bags Mark had first seen at the Zoffany studios. They were young people, all very attractive, all smiling, dressed in MZTV T-shirts and caps, laughing and joking with the crowd.

"Oh, there's Leila and Gary," Sarah Watkins was saying, but Mark was pushing forward through the outer fringes of the crowd for a closer look at the young men and women on the stand.

People all around him shoved and jostled to grab their free bags of merchandise. Many had already done so. A girl almost elbowed Mark in the eye as she struggled into a blue T-shirt. A young kid waved a plastic phoenix toy in his face.

"Hey, the world looks great this way!" The voice cracked loudly, close by. Mark turned and saw a husband and wife wearing MZTV trick spectacles. The flimsy plastic lenses were mirrored to make them look like flashing TV screens.

Mark shuddered and barged rudely past them.

But what caused him the greatest unease was the small group up on the platform. From a distance they did indeed resemble film stars, glamorous and smiling. Closer in, Mark could see the thick makeup they all wore: greasepaint giving their skins a slightly waxy sheen; hair that looked as though it had been dyed; eyebrows a little too thickly penciled in; teeth that were just a shade too white and perfect.

The thought slid into Mark's mind as he remembered last night's ordeal – what's underneath all that makeup? *What do those people really look like?*

"Hi, Mark, how'ya doing?"

Mark turned as Gary flashed a pair of MZTV specs in front of his eyes. He brushed them aside. Two steps behind her brother, Leila made an expression of disapproval at Gary's antics.

"This is pretty good, eh? You've got to admit, MZTV is really trying to grab the public's attention. There's all kinds of cool stuff in this bag."

Mark noticed that Leila had no freebie bag in her hand.

"I see you're not tempted."

She looked past Mark and sneered at the people on the stage.

"It's cheap and nasty. Look at that – even little kids are wearing the stuff. You ought to know better, Gary," she chided him. "Especially after what's happened."

"We don't even know MZTV is involved," he countered. "Has Roy been in touch about it?"

"No," Leila admitted. "He hasn't." She started moving away from the crowd, leaving Gary to it. Mark followed her to a quieter spot where some benches were set facing a stand of ornamental trees. They sat down together.

"He's really juvenile sometimes," Leila sighed. Mark grinned. "Oh, Gary's okay. He just gets carried away with new things: toys and gadgets. Look how he is with his computer."

"I suppose so." She stared at Mark darkly. "But he's right about Roy. He hasn't phoned or anything."

"We only saw him yesterday afternoon…" Mark hesitated. He felt the urge to tell Leila about last night's encounter at the studios; felt the urge to depend on her, just as Sarah needed to depend on him. But a promise was a promise, so he let the moment pass.

"Anyway," Leila said, waving as she saw Mrs. Watkins approaching the supermarket entrance, "how is your Mom?"

Mark shrugged. "Pretending that Tina will walk in through the door at any moment."

"There's a difference, you know, between true hope and just kidding yourself. Your mother's not stupid."

The look in Leila's eyes and the expression on her face were so intense that Mark found he couldn't bear them. "I'd better go," he told her. "I said I'd help with the groceries."

He almost stumbled away from her as tears prickled in his eyes – turned and nearly collided with the thing that rushed up toward him.

"MZTV – MZTV – it's the only one for me!"

Gary was wearing the full kit: blue phoenix T-shirt, cap with logo, shiny badges and decals, and the glasses that made his face look empty and vague. He was waggling his head to and fro, singing along to a tape playing on a personal stereo. And even that, Mark noticed, gleamed with a blue metallized finish and the Zoffany Studio logo.

"You got *that* for free?" Mark wondered, as Gary pushed by him and skipped along, still singing his silly, pointless song.

"Mark, Mark, are you coming or not?" Sarah Watkins called from the supermarket's entrance.

But Mark was staring after his friend, his face darkening with concern.

"MZTV – MZTV – it's the only one for me…"

"Gary – Gary!" Mark yelled, while the thought came, quite unbidden – *That doesn't seem like Gary at all.*

Chapter 11

After fussing all evening, Leila's parents at last stepped out onto the porch, Mrs. Swann drawing her coat around her shoulders while her husband went to back the car out of the garage. The night was chilly, the streetlights turned into chalky smudges by the heaviest fog that autumn.

"Now, we're only a mile away, so if you need anything – "

"Mom, you've said all this." Leila tried hard to keep the impatience out of her voice.

"And you've got – "

"Yes, Mom, I've got the Scotts's number if I need to call you."

"And when Gary comes home – "

"I'll call you right away when he gets back."

Mrs. Swann smiled in a way that failed to conceal her unease. Gary had not come home from the mall with his sister and – it was quite unlike him – he hadn't called to say where he was. Leila had contacted Mark first, and then Gary's other few close friends, but none of them had seen him.

"Well, that's teenagers for you!" Mrs. Swann said in sudden frustration, as though forgetting that Leila was exactly the same age as her twin brother.

Leila smiled at that and hugged her mom. "Listen, don't worry. He's got involved in some computer game somewhere – probably down at The Arcade. Shall I bike over and – "

"No, don't do that. I don't want both of you

wandering around on such a foggy night."

"Just enjoy yourself, Mom. You haven't been to a dinner party in ages."

"How can I enjoy myself when – "

The loud blare of the car's horn interrupted them. "Oh, your father gets so impatient!"

Mrs. Swann kissed her daughter on the cheek. "Mrs. Lumley next door will keep an eye on you."

"Oh, that means she'll see all the boys arriving with their cans of beer and – "

Leila laughed at her mother's look of shock.

"Just joking. Have a wonderful time."

She watched her parents drive away, the car's red taillights dwindling into the fog. She shivered, then went inside.

Although Leila understood her mother's anxiety over Gary, she didn't share it. He was just that kind of person, letting himself get carried away with things, just as Mark had said earlier. And her own hunch was probably correct: at that moment Gary was most likely beating everyone's high score down on the video game machines in The Arcade. He had money in his pocket and would probably take a taxi home.

Leila made herself some toast and coffee, then went into the living room. She'd brought a paperback down from her bedroom, but found she couldn't concentrate, so tossed it onto the side table by the armchair and flicked on the television with the remote.

The screen shimmered into life, the picture immediately tearing into shreds. Actors' faces twisted and melted, sliding sideways, while the whole image rolled slowly down toward the bottom of the screen.

Leila changed channels, searching first through all of her regular ones, then moving on to scan others she rarely watched. Every one of them showed the same scrambled screen: a picture savaged by lightning and hissing static spitting from the speakers.

She dropped the remote in irritation, wondering if the aerial cable had come loose. That would explain the loss of picture. Or maybe it was just the fog, or something.

She pushed herself out of the armchair and walked across the room to the TV in the corner. She leaned over the set, smelling its dry, plasticky heat, and peered behind.

The black aerial cable had indeed come loose: Leila could see the metal connector lying on the carpet. But – and her skin crawled as she noticed this – another cable had been fitted into the TV. This one had a blue flex, while the connection socket was a bright and gleaming silver.

She reached toward it –

And the new blue cable writhed like a snake at her touch.

She screamed once, briefly, before a wave of tingling energy flung her backward, sprawling onto the carpet.

Leila's head spun, her body echoing painfully with the shock. Through a haze of dizziness she saw the cable thrashing about at the back of the TV, its other end vanishing down through the floor, while on the screen a blizzard of pixels swarmed behind the glass.

Then they seemed to sweep together, whirling into a ghostly form that reached out to her with hands as vague and pale as the October fog outside.

A face took shape, composed of snowy dots. The eyes, lost and terrified, were made of flickering particles.

"*Leila*", "it said, like the whispering of dust at the window, "*Leila, help me…*"

"Gary!" The cry broke like the crack of a dry stick from the girl's throat. She struggled to stand, took a faltering step toward the screen – then stopped as she saw, or imagined she saw, the dreadful dark shadow hovering behind Gary's phantom form. It was a shadow dragged from some unimaginably cold and evil place, a shadow that did not belong here, in this world where people lived and the sun shone. It came from elsewhere, an alien thing.

"Oh, Gary, no…"

As the image of her brother wavered, its almost-voice pleading mournfully from far away, Leila backed slowly toward the living room door. She had no idea what was happening, and hardly any of what she could do about it. But maybe Mark would know. She could trust him. She could rely on him…

Only when her hand touched the jamb of the doorway behind her did Leila feel able to turn her back on the TV screen. Then she started to run the ten yards that would take her out of the house and to safety.

Halfway along the hall was the telephone table, and beside that a door beneath the stairs that led down to the cellar...

A needle of brilliant light was blazing from the keyhole of that door; and even as Leila watched, the angle of the light shifted; there came a busy rustling against the wood – and then the door burst outward in a blinding cascade of white light.

☠

The light washed toward Leila and crashed over her – *and through her* – tingling along every nerve, spilling a kaleidoscope of pictures into her brain. She screamed again for a second time, feeling her senses slipping away, panicking now that she would be drawn down into this nightmare and be turned into a faint and pathetic ghost, as her brother had been.

Only the dread of that happening lent her the strength to fight back. Like someone drowning in a stormy sea, Leila battled through the dazzling, hissing chaos, giving a final, desperate push –

And staggered clear of the light on its far side. She looked back briefly. The radiance was now splashing against the walls, up as high as the hallway ceiling, churning like glowing foam across the floor. And more of it was pouring up from the cellar in shining clouds, followed by an even greater brightness, if that were possible.

A brightness in the shape of a man.

There was a face somewhere deep amid the incandescence, and eyes, and a voice that was trying to speak to her. But there was no heart, and no human soul in that light. Right at the core of it, she knew, lay the Shadow…

Leila didn't listen to the words of the Shadow whispering softly in her mind. Instead she wrenched open the front door and ran out into the night.

Her immediate aim was just to get away, but beyond the porch she saw Gary's bike leaning against the side fence where he'd left it – and for once she blessed his carelessness that had left the bike unlocked.

She heaved it around, leaped into the seat and sped down the driveway, her feet churning the pedals, her leg muscles burning with effort.

At the bottom of the driveway, as she brought the bike around in a controlled skid to face up the street, Leila glanced over her shoulder. The whole house was ablaze with the silver fire, which streamed from every window and chink, streaking in all directions until it faded into dense, pearly distances.

And as she watched, just a moment later, a spark seemed to snap in the house next door – the Lumleys' home – and the same light erupted inside.

Trembling, Leila pumped more energy into her legs to increase her speed. The bike's tires sizzled on the night-damp road; her hair streamed out behind her and the cold air burned icily against her face. She had never cycled so fast in her life.

But even so, the light kept pace, leaping like flames from house to house, filling each house in a second, so that Leila's speeding shadow was stamped anew, moment by moment, on the road.

The end of the street was in sight now, and beyond that lay the busy main road. There she would find people, traffic, police patrol cars…

Leila put on a final spurt – and so was quite unable to stop when a manhole cover in the road ahead exploded upward and spun like a dull coin high in the air.

And from out of the hole rose a mass of writhing, glowing cables – one of which snaked quickly toward her and entangled itself among the spokes of the bicycle's front wheel.

Chapter 12

Leila felt a savage jolt. The bike stopped instantly, pitching her over the handlebars. There was an instant's dizziness and fear, and then she slammed hard, on her left side, into the road.

Pain flared through her like fire, followed by the secondary discomfort of the bike tumbling over her back and coming to rest a few feet away, the wheels spinning lazily.

Leila curled around the agony in her left arm, becoming aware that the tangle of silvery cables was moving toward her – one cable extending more quickly than the others, reaching for her face. For her eyes.

She tried to twist herself clear, whimpering as she moved her arm, and confused now because the night was filling with light and a roaring sound that suddenly stopped –

Then there were voices – voices she knew – and clattering footsteps.

Hands hooked themselves under her arms and began to drag her clear. She saw Roy Case, a horrified look on his face, leap for the wriggling cable. He grabbed it as he might have grabbed a dangerous snake, heaved it around to the gutter and thrust it deep into the drain.

A spectacular flash lit up the night, and a sound like water poured onto a hotplate. Showers of blue sparks sprayed high into the air, like fireworks. Leila watched them in a kind of wonder as they reached the apex of their flight,

74

and then started to drift quietly down, fading one by one until all but a few were extinguished. Then those, too, the brightest ones, blinked out.

Ten left…six…two…

The final spark faded and Leila's mind turned toward a warm and welcoming darkness.

☠

She woke to see Mark's worried face in front of her. It rippled, as though she were seeing it through water. She tried to smile, to show him she was all right – that she had survived. But somehow her body seemed distant and strange, and she wasn't sure if the smile had worked properly at all.

Mark turned and spoke some words. They were plain and simple words, but oddly difficult to understand right now.

Leila tried to see who he was talking to. The blackness was moving in and out, all around her. Someone else spoke then, with a deeper voice, but equally concerned for her, it appeared.

A cool hand pressed against her forehead. "She's blacking out again," the voice said – and Leila felt elated to recognize it as Roy's.

Then the enveloping blackness moved in, so far it covered her completely: hands, feet, eyes, thoughts…everything.

She snapped awake, realizing things had changed. Now she was inside somewhere, but could still see out into the street. Various people were walking around, and a police patrol car was parked nearby, its red and blue warning lights flickering. Another car had been positioned sideways, to block the road. Police officers seemed to be searching front gardens with flashlights.

Leila shifted herself for a better view, and found that she was lying on a soft surface – a bed – and had been covered by a light metallic sheet that crackled as she moved. Her left arm would not move at all: it had been strapped securely to her side.

"Leila – " Mark said.

The world bounced softly as Mark stood up in the ambulance. A paramedic standing just outside the open rear doors stepped in. Roy followed just afterward.

"She's come around…Leila, are you okay?"

She turned to look at Mark, wincing at a new twinge in her shoulder.

"I'm…" She observed herself carefully as she said it. "I'm fine. And have I got a story to tell you!"

Roy leaned over her, beaming. "Glad you're back with us, honey…but wait just a moment. I have a few friends who would like to listen to that story just as much as I would."

He disappeared for a moment, then returned with two uniformed policemen.

"Leila, this is Sergeant Holmes." Roy indicated the older of the two, then pointed to the younger officer, who stood behind Holmes by the door. "And this is Officer Connor."

"We were patrolling along the North Road," Holmes told Leila. His rather lined and leathery

76

face wrinkled into a reassuring smile. "We saw some strange flashes of light above the houses here – and at just about the same time all hell broke loose on the police radio. Isn't that right, Bob?"

Officer Connor nodded briskly, pushing a shaky hand through his straight, dark hair. He looked strained and tired by the evening's events.

"Right enough, Sarge. People were phoning headquarters from all over the city, reporting similar unusual flares and flashes. At first we thought something had happened at the power company – but they were as much in the dark as we were."

Holmes chuckled. "'In the dark' says it all. *No one* seems to know what's been going on."

"So it's very important you try to remember everything that happened to you, Leila," Roy said, sitting on the edge of the bed. "Because unless we can fully understand this mystery, it's bound to get worse."

"I'll do my best," Leila answered. She frowned. "But how come you arrived just as that – " she laughed nervously as she remembered, " – that cable got caught in my bike wheels?"

"It was me." Mark looked a little self-conscious as he said it. "I was worrying about Gary, after you called me…I was worrying about you, too, Leila. I called Roy, and we decided to drive around to, um, tell you a few things."

Leila noticed Mark's expression as he glanced at Roy, as though they shared a secret between them that nobody else knew about, not even Sergeant Holmes.

"Anyway, as we pulled into the street, we saw what was happening."

"You were just in time…" Leila's voice was very quiet, and trembling as she recalled her experience in the house. "If the cable had reached me – touched me – I might have turned into…into…"

"It's all right." Roy squeezed her hand. "Start right at the beginning, and take it slowly. You've got all the time in the world."

After she had finished, there was a long silence. Police officers and a few paramedics were still searching gardens and houses along the street, but it was clear that the examination had revealed no explanation. People were starting to pack up and leave. One or two cars were driving away into the drifting fog.

It was obvious to Leila that Sergeant Holmes and the younger cop hadn't believed a word of it. And indeed, even as she'd related her vision of Gary's ghostly face on the TV screen, and then that terrible creature of light coming out of the cellar, it sounded incredible to Leila also. If she had not been able to glimpse the dead cables lying in a charred sprawl outside the ambulance, she'd have admitted the whole thing was nothing more than a dreadful nightmare.

But the cable *was* there, jumbled like a burned and monstrous octopus, the ends disappearing down through the manhole in the road. And she *had* seen Gary's face – or something like it – and the Shadow *had* reached out and touched her soul with its black and icy finger.

"I did not make this up," Leila added, her

voice now strong and determined.

"Sarge," Officer Connor interrupted, "I guess we've got to believe the girl." He had just finished speaking to another policeman who'd whispered something up to him from outside.

Holmes's craggy brow furrowed. "How come?"

"Because Officer Grove tells me the search teams have been through every house in the street – and nobody was found in any of them. They've all vanished, Sarge. Every single man, woman, and child has disappeared."

☠

Roy Case pulled up outside his apartment block with a sigh. He did not like the car he'd rented, but his own would be under repair for a week or more. Mark, sitting beside him, looked pale and weary at the end of this long day. In the rear seat, Leila was already asleep.

"We'll wake her in a few minutes," Roy said. "Let's go up and check my apartment first – let's check the whole block, in fact."

It took twenty minutes, and in that time Roy and Mark asked nearly all of the residents if they'd maybe seen or heard anything unusual. All seemed quiet.

As they came out through the lobby and began walking toward Roy's car, two other cars turned off the road and drew up. Sarah Watkins stepped out of one, Carl and Renata Swann, Leila's parents, from the other.

Roy sighed again. He had suggested the plan

himself, though wondered now if he'd live to regret it.

"Let me help you with your bags." He turned toward Sarah, but Mrs. Swann reached him first and thrust a heavy, bulging suitcase into his hands. Of course, it would be much safer this way, but –

"We'll have to arrange shifts for the bathroom," Mrs. Swann was saying. "And to take our showers. But we all agree, Mr. Case, it's much better if we stay together until this terrible business is over. Obviously *something* has come into our home and taken my little Gary away…"

She started to sniffle. Carl Swann offered his wife a handkerchief and shook his head slowly.

Roy sighed for a third time and struggled back toward the apartment building, the huge suitcase banging painfully against his shins.

80

Chapter 13

Everyone went to bed late that night, once the apartment had been rearranged to house so many people. Roy, Mark, and Leila were the last to turn in; they had just finished washing the dinner dishes. Mark draped the tea towel over its rack by the stove, stretched his arms, and yawned. Leila dropped the last few knives and forks into the cutlery drawer.

"I feel so useless," she said, glancing at her injured left arm. The paramedic who'd treated her said the limb had to be kept strapped up for a week at least.

Mark shrugged. "No need. I don't mind washing the dishes – though if you ask me to cook it'd be a different story!"

"I wouldn't inflict that on anyone," Leila chuckled, again disconcerting Mark by the warmth and brightness of her smile. He did not know – and had never known – quite how to handle that smile, and was almost glad of the excuse to look away as the door opened and Roy came in. He was wearing slippers and a bathrobe, and looked utterly unlike the famous TV detective people were so used to seeing on screen.

"Is Mom okay?" Mark asked.

"She's fine, sleeping now," Roy said. "And I've just left your parents, Leila. I assured them that I'd spare no effort in finding Gary, just as I won't rest until we find Tina safe and well. And to be honest, I think that when we discover one, we'll also discover the other. They've both been taken by the same thing – by the same *force*."

"Max Zoffany Television…" Leila said it as though the words tasted foul in her mouth.

Roy nodded. "Or whatever is using MZTV as a cover to draw people into its trap. Because it's quite clear that something terrible is happening in Kenniston – something that's centered around MZTV, but that is quickly spreading."

"All over the city?"

"Not quite, not yet. Sergeant Holmes was saying that the street where you live, Leila, has been affected the worst. It was almost as if the force, or whatever was controlling that force, was chasing you – "

"Because I suspect the link with Zoffany?"

"Could be," Roy said. "And it would also account for your unpleasant experience with the Carpenters next door, Mark. Maybe they were keeping an eye on you, to see how our investigation progressed."

"So why did *lots* of people vanish tonight?" Mark wanted to know.

"For reasons we don't yet understand – "

"And why," Leila interrupted, "hasn't the force that came after us tried to capture you, Roy, or worse?"

Roy Case grinned unexpectedly, surprising them both. "You'd make great detectives," he said. The smile waned. "And you'll need to be, in the days to come. Because, now that Gary has gone also, the job is too big for me to handle alone."

"But the police – " Mark began.

"Are already rushed off their feet with this wave of disappearances. Besides, you heard Tony Holmes and Connor: they don't believe a word of it. Nobody will believe us until it's way too late. So, tomorrow we'll take things a step further. I'll take you with me to SBTV: there's some equipment I want to pick up, and we'll also have a chance to discuss our plans."

"Mom'll be happy, knowing I'm in safe hands."

"My parents, too," Leila said. She stared at Roy. "But you didn't answer my question – how come the force hasn't attacked you yet?"

Roy walked over to the counter, opened the coffee jar, and tipped two heaping spoonfuls of coffee granules into a mug.

"I have no idea," he admitted. "Though I guess I'll stay up awhile longer and think about it."

☠

The next day dawned sunny and fine, the cloying fog of the previous night having vanished without a trace. Mark and Leila arose early, then made coffee and toast for their parents while Roy shaved and showered. They were out of the house and halfway across town in Roy's rented car by 8:30.

"It's amazing," Leila said, gazing around at the towering office buildings, their top floors glittering in the sunlight. "But you'd never know that anything was wrong…It all looks so normal, and all of these people are going about their business quite unaware."

"It's because Zoffany is being very clever, very sly," Mark commented, "keeping his scheme underground – "

Roy slammed on the brakes. "What did you say?"

"Um…I think Zoffany's keeping his plans hidden until he's ready…"

"'Underground.' You said 'underground'! Why didn't I think of that earlier!"

Motorists honked their horns behind Roy's car; he waved cheerfully and moved away again.

"It's obvious now – that whole episode last night with the cables, Leila…"

"I'll never forget it!" She shuddered.

"But don't you see – the cables that attacked you were *fiber-optic cables*, the kind of cables that TV pictures are sent along, instead of being broadcast through the air. The cables we saw, and goodness knows how many others, are being controlled by the same force that's created Zoffany's TV studios out of the wasteland. The force that is our enemy is causing TV cables to grow through the ground, like the roots of some terrible tree. Nobody knows where it's happening, or even that it *is* happening – until the cables connect themselves to television sets."

"And then," added Mark, "all hell breaks loose."

☠

The Solid Broadcast building came into view. Roy parked the car in the basement parking lot, and the three took the elevator to Andy Hitchman's control room on the fifth floor. A number of SBTV technicians and personnel waved hello to Roy, one of them coming across to whisper a word in his ear.

Both Mark and Leila saw Roy's expression change as he heard the news.

"Problems?" Leila asked. Roy was frowning.

"Not sure. Pete was just saying that Andy had a letter from MZTV in his mail this morning. He didn't say what it was about, but Andy went straight to his office and hasn't been seen since. The rumor is that Zoffany's making a takeover bid for Solid Broadcast."

"But he can't just come along and *buy* the place!" Mark was aghast.

Roy was about to reply when they were all startled by shouting and commotion in the control room.

The striplights in the ceiling buzzed and dimmed suddenly, then fluttered back into life. But the control consoles nearby were going crazy and, to everyone's amazement, the bank of TV screens built into one wall blanked out and then brightened again – but now every single one of them was showing MZTV programs.

Chapter 14

A few moments later, Andy Hitchman came storming out of his office.

"What the heck is going on around here? How come the TV on my desk is…"

His voice trailed away as his stride faltered. Everyone in the control room had fallen silent. The striplights had taken on an eerie sheen, like moonlight seen through thin clouds. Puzzled faces were turning toward the old movie playing on all the screens in the room. It looked as though it had come right out of the 1940s – a smartly dressed couple stood on a balcony overlooking the sea at sunset. The man had brilliantined black hair, combed back, and was wearing a tuxedo; the woman beside him wore a shimmery evening gown, her long hair knotted elaborately and threaded with pearls. Violins were playing sweetly in the background.

"Sylvia," the man was saying huskily, "I love you so much…I will always love you – until the end of time."

"Oh, Gordon," sighed the lady, looking up adoringly into his eyes, "you mean so much to me!"

"Darling – " Gordon bent toward her. "Kiss me, kiss me now, my love, my sweet…"

"Oh, *please*!" Mark exclaimed. Andy Hitchman was still staring open-mouthed at the screens.

"But this is awful!" he declared. "Who watches such nonsense these days?"

Leila cocked her head at the chic couple and

smiled. "I think it's rather cute…That's how people were then."

"*Then*," Hitchman said with emphasis. "Not now. How come MZTV can get away with broadcasting such – such junk? *And how come they've tapped into our transmissions?*" He turned to one of his technicians. "Jack, get up on the roof, will you, and check out the tower. And Roy – you're the famous detective around here, so find out who's doing this to us!"

Roy nodded. The couple in the movie had their arms around each other and were gazing out to sea. The violins had reached a crescendo, and "The End" appeared in glowing letters above them.

The film faded to black, and another, seemingly just like it, started immediately afterward. Hitchman groaned.

"I don't think they'll find anything on the roof," Leila whispered urgently to Roy and Mark.

"I agree," Roy said. "Let's go down to the basement."

☠

The elevator took them to the lower ground floor, which was the SBTV parking lot. From there, a flight of stone steps led to an even lower level, a place that seemed to be a mass of tunnels, pipes, and electrical wiring. The place was hot and dimly lit, and as soon as the three reached the bottom of the steps, they could smell the bitter stink of scorching in the air.

Roy wrinkled his nose. "Something's not right

here...Torrance, the caretaker, ought to be around somewhere. He should have reported this problem."

If he's able to, Leila thought, but said nothing to the others.

Roy took a flashlight from his inside jacket pocket and flicked it on: the thin, bright beam penetrated the stuffy gloom of the basement corridor. Water pipes and air-conditioning conduits ran along the ceiling; clusters of multicolored wires were bracketed to the walls. The smell of scorching grew stronger.

"Maybe we ought to call the fire department," Mark suggested nervously. The air was becoming increasingly unpleasant, and pearls of sweat were appearing on the faces of all three of them.

"There isn't any fire down here," Roy replied, with a strange cast to his voice.

"The studio is too valuable to burn down."

"Too valuable? To who?"

"I think we all know who." Leila glanced at Mark squarely. "The only question is, has Zoffany actually gained control yet?"

Up ahead, the steamy gloom was glowing fitfully as something dimmed and brightened around the next corner. And they heard a fizzing, crackling sound now, as of busy lightning skimming along metal surfaces. There was a footstep, then a scuffling, then a cloud of eerie whisperings, swiftly vanishing into silence.

"Looks like this is it," Roy said quietly. "Get ready to run, guys."

They edged cautiously forward to the corner

and peered around.

The walls were alive with writhing optical cable. It had pushed up from below ground, cracking through the concrete, clinging like vines to the walls, the ceiling – and to Torrance.

He burst into brilliance as Roy, Mark, and Leila first caught sight of him, transformed into a creature of light in an instant. The longest cable was jammed into his mouth, but now he pulled it free and swung to face the newcomers.

Torrance's eyes were a storm of sparks, and tiny tendrils of electricity rippled inside his mouth as he spoke: *"I love you so much...I will always love you - until the end of time..."*

Then he shambled forward, holding the spitting cable-end out in front of him.

Mark and Leila dove sideways in opposite directions as Torrance thrust the cable toward them. But Roy, perhaps thinking he could defeat the man or even reason with him, stood his ground and snatched at Torrance's arm.

The air tore through with a noise like sheet lightning. Roy was hurled backward, hitting the stone floor heavily some yards away, then sliding along on his back until he struck the far wall, where he lay still, his eyes closed. Smoke curled upward from his half-open mouth. His hands twitched spasmodically.

It had all happened so fast that Mark and Leila had no time to react. But now, as Torrance paused in his attack, they were able to realize their danger. Torrance smiled, the light that spilled from his jaws causing the shadows to shift and dance all around him.

Mark looked across and saw the fear on Leila's face. With panic mounting inside him, he searched for a weapon.

Torrance played a few yards of the living cable through his hands – *those terrible hands, like bloody glass* – and began to lash it in front of himself like a whip, its tip spurting sparks that seemed to scorch the air itself. The smell of burning was now very intense.

Leila backed off carefully, a step at a time. But Mark dove forward, within range of the whirling cable, and snatched a fire extinguisher from its bracket on the wall. With shaking fingers, he ripped the lockpin free, aimed the nozzle, and squeezed the trigger.

A gush of white dry-ice vapor poured and billowed out, completely blocking his view, and Leila's, sending Torrance reeling back with an unearthly shriek that quickly faded to silence. But within the cloud, the glowing and fitfull glittering continued, growing brighter and brighter until Torrance came rushing toward Mark and Leila with a raw scream of pure animal rage.

And behind him and around him, the incandescent cables twined and quested like the many-headed Hydra.

"Get out! Get out now!" Mark yelled to Leila as he stumbled backward. He heaved the heavy extinguisher into Torrance's face - then turned around and ran.

A cable flashed forward and, rising up like a striking cobra, spat a gout of fire at the boy. It struck the wall nearby and splashed liquid flame across the brickwork to his left. Mark hurled himself to the right, crashing into the opposite wall of the corridor. Another ball of flame flew close by his head, striking the ground near to where Roy lay and burning there brightly for a few dazzling seconds.

Leila was aware that whatever was directing the cable was finding its aim: the next firebolt would surely strike one or the other of her friends and set them on fire. There seemed to be no way out of the trap…

Except perhaps for one.

She acted without thinking, without bothering to work anything out. It was a desperate move and she did it out of pure instinct – tearing off her jacket, scooping it through the pool of flames on the floor, then flinging the burning thing up toward the ceiling.

It brushed by a small detector, that immediately activated a flashing red light and a high-pitched klaxon sound. The fire alarm device also triggered the sprinkler system.

All along the corridor, water jets snapped on, spraying a fine rain down over Mark, Roy, Leila herself, and the squirming web of tentacles that whipped and thrashed furiously as they drew back, dripping, into the darkness.

Last of all, the cable that Torrance had used as a weapon flopped to the concrete floor and trembled as though dying. The light ebbed from within it until finally it lay motionless, while nearby, Torrance the caretaker, his skin white and his eyes glazed, slumped to his knees and fell forward with a groan, unconscious.

Chapter 15

While Leila rushed over to tend to Roy, Mark very cautiously walked back along the corridor. He stooped to check on Torrance: the man was out cold, but was alive and seemed to have suffered no permanent harm. Just beyond him, the thick, jumbled strands of fiber-optic cable reached away into the dimness.

Mark traced them as far as he could, hardly daring to move into the shadows. After what had happened to Leila the day before, he – all three of them – had become wary of shadowy places, nervous of the dark. But as he stared, Mark was mildly surprised to see that the gloom did not deepen ahead: in fact, it grew brighter, with a pale white light cast along the wall.

Perhaps Torrance had a little cubby-hole office there, and the light had been left on. Maybe he was watching TV when he was attacked.

Mark giggled uneasily at the thought. He took his courage in both hands and moved forward, craning his neck to check out his ideas.

What he saw sent a shock of panic through him.

A gleaming cable as thick as his arm had pushed up through the floor, straight up the wall,and then through the ceiling. It was pulsing with incredible energy – Mark was tempted to say with unnatural life – as it delivered its evil message to the floors above…to the control room.

Mark dashed back to Leila. He found Roy sitting upright, looking dazed, rubbing at a bad bruise on his forehead.

"We didn't kill it!" Mark yelled urgently, jabbing his finger toward the flight of steps. "There's another cable – it's gone through the roof – come on, it's taking over the studio!"

☠

Roy scrambled up and followed the teenagers as they leaped up the steps and ran for the elevator. He slipped between the doors as they swished closed.

From the way the light in the ceiling dimmed and flared, they knew that the cable must be draining enormous power from the system. Or perhaps it was deliberately trying to black out SBTV transmissions, so that Zoffany could flood the city with his own programs – those sad, weird movies from a bygone time.

The elevator juddered to a stop at the fifth floor, the servo motors whining as the doors drew open erratically.

Roy looked out into the control room – and a chair smashed into the wall beside him, shattering to sticks and splinters.

The place was in chaos, with technicians fighting one another, seemingly for no reason…until Mark spotted the empty glare in one tech's eyes, and knew that what had happened to Torrance was also happening to them.

"The force is inside the machinery," Leila whispered fearfully. "And it's getting into the people."

"Just like the Carpenters," Mark added, "and the families along your street, Leila. The force touches them somehow, turns them into puppets – into TV zombies!"

Roy nodded. "That must be it. The images broadcast by Zoffany are laced with this evil energy. If you gaze at the TV screen too long, then you fall under its spell. Those dreadful old movies must be like camouflage: behind them is a much more sinister message – "

"Sent by Zoffany."

"Or by something worse, Mark." The thought came to Roy's mind unbidden, and unwelcome. "Or by something much, much worse."

When Leila pressed the elevator button, it wouldn't work. And now the lights were fizzling out, though the room's many TV screens still blazed brilliantly.

"The cable is draining the electrical power," Roy said. He pushed Mark and Leila from the elevator and crouched with them behind a desk. Nearby, one of the control room staff threw his hands up to his face with a shriek. Then he let them drop loosely. The three were horrified to see that his eyes had changed into something not quite human.

The technician picked up a length of wood and advanced on someone who, a moment ago, had been his friend...

"Stay here!" Roy commanded. He jumped up and threw himself into the fight, smashing against the technician from behind and crashing down with him to the floor.

"What does he mean, 'Stay here'?" Leila's fists were clenched in frustration.

"Solid Broadcast is being taken over, and he wants us to cower like a couple of helpless kids!"

"Well, we *are* kids," Mark pointed out wryly.

"But we're not helpless – and I for one intend to prove it!"

She started to rise, but Mark grabbed her elbow and pulled her back. "Leila, why is it so dark now?"

"The lights – " she began. Mark was shaking his head.

"But the sun was shining when we arrived, less than half an hour ago."

There were no windows in the room, but together they glanced up at the skylight and saw solid blackness beyond –

Blackness that was suddenly dispelled, for a split second, by a flicker of lightning.

"The transmission tower," Leila breathed. "That's what the force wants. All of this is just a diversion."

Impulsively, the teenagers hugged each other. Then together they stood and prepared to battle their way to the emergency stairs.

☠

As far as they could, they stumbled away from the unfortunates who had been possessed, using cover where possible to avoid flying furniture and debris. Halfway to the stairs, Leila noticed the fire alarm, and wondered if they could try the same trick again, and set it off.

Even as the thought occurred to her, a blank-faced man whose eyes rippled with TV-light barred their way. He roared at them, his mouth a network of blue electrical threads. They backed off, dodging behind a console, then bolted the last few yards to the stairs.

Echoes bounced around them from the bare walls. It was completely black in the stairwell, except when lightning streaked across the sky outside; then for an instant they could see each other and the way ahead. But every time the lightning came, a boom of thunder followed, resounding through the building and causing Mark and Leila to clamp their hands to their ears in pain and fear.

After what seemed like many minutes, Mark's outstretched hands felt the cold metal of the door that led to the roof. He searched madly for the handle, tugged and twisted it, then pushed his shoulder to the door and with difficulty shoved it open.

A gust of icy wind cut into him, swirling rain into his eyes. He cried out as the storm of droplets lashed his face. Just behind him, Leila shivered.

"There's a gale blowing up here!" Mark yelled. He heaved the door open further and squeezed out onto the wide expanse of the building's flat roof.

Leila followed, gasping as the howling wind numbed her body and the downpour drenched her hair.

Standing close together, the two found their

bearings. Beyond a squat, square generator room, the TV transmission tower thrust into the sky, its pinnacle hidden among the streaming clouds. Beyond, the storm-smeared shapes of other office buildings and high-rises rippled into the distance. But amazingly, toward the horizon, the sky was still blue and the sun was still shining – as though the real world still existed beyond the edges of this nightmare.

Leila leaned close to speak into Mark's ear. "Do you think the cable is inside the generator room?"

Mark shrugged. "Who knows? We'll try the door. If it's locked, well – there must be some way of forcing it open! Come on!"

He went ahead of Leila, both of them pressing themselves to the wall of the power room to keep out of the worst of the rain.

Reaching the corner, Mark turned and grinned nervously at his companion, then stepped into the storm's full blast.

A jagged pitchfork of lightning jabbed overhead. And in its light, Leila saw a hand flash out and clamp itself around Mark's throat.

Chapter 16

Mark did not see it coming so had no chance to dodge its awful grip. The power of his attacker's hand was amazing, and within a few seconds Mark felt himself blacking out, as the pressure inside his head built up to an unendurable pitch.

Leila shrank back against the wall – it was a reflex action of which she was instantly ashamed. She realized quickly that Mark was in a life-and-death situation. Obviously his foe was far too strong to be fought alone. And so, conquering her fear, she leaped forward into the brunt of the storm, and into full view of Mark's opponent.

There was no recognition of her in Andy Hitchman's expression, and precious little humanity. His eyes held that same, frightful, pearly light she had seen in all the others controlled by the force: the light of blind hatred and blind obedience. And the man's skin was as white as sun-bleached bones, embroidered by filaments of tiny lightning that quivered like living cobwebs along his arm and over Mark's face.

Seeing this, Leila gave a yell of rage and alarm. She grasped Hitchman's forearm with her right hand, her only usable hand, and tried to drag him off – but his muscles felt like steel cable and the sting of the energy pouring through him forced her to let go.

Hitchman gave a wild animal growl and pulled Mark closer. Leila ran at him in a panic; because Mark's eyes had closed and he was starting now to sag into unconsciousness.

Hitchman's other arm swung up and smashed into Leila's shoulder. It felt like being hit with a baseball bat. She tumbled through the air and crashed down onto her back, the rain streaming over her in a ceaseless torrent.

But then she noticed that Hitchman was not coming after her: he was staying close to the sheltering wall of the power house, *out of the worst of the rain*. Leila remembered how Torrance had been returned to normal by the sprinkler system in the basement. Obviously Hitchman – or the force that was directing him – could be badly affected by water, perhaps in the way that electrical machinery could be short-circuited.

Even as the idea occurred to her, Leila knew it must be true. And so, though her body was a mass of aches and bruises, and though a voice inside her head was screaming for her to stop, Leila scrambled up and ran directly at the thing that had been Andy Hitchman.

She hit him at full speed, causing him to crash back against the wall. Mark slipped from his grasp – which was the opportunity Leila had hoped for.

Now, as he reached for her, she seized his hand and jerked her body backward, using all of her weight and strength to drag him, off balance, into the deluge.

Hitchman had no time to think, no chance to resist. A powerful gust sprayed a shower of raindrops across him. He bellowed like a wounded bull...

But Leila kept tugging him further out onto

100

the roof, changing her angle to swing him around. Then she pushed, hard, and sent him staggering back into a deep and wind-lashed puddle. He splashed into the middle of it, threw up his hands and slumped to his knees.

The network of lightning shimmering over his body seemed to gather then and surge upward into his head. Hitchman's eyes brightened until they were too brilliant to look into -

And he shrieked in absolute agony.

It was a sound unlike any that Leila had heard in her life before: a sound that went on and on, rising up over Andy Hitchman to a point a foot or so above his head. At that point the lightning gathered, each thread weaving itself into a single rippling red shape that writhed in brief torment, before streaking away into the tumbled black sky with a howl.

Hitchman fell face forward into the puddle, and lay still.

Leila tended to him quickly, turning him over to make sure he was still alive, before she hurried to Mark. He was starting to come around, his eyes trying to focus.

"L-Leila…" His voice sounded weary and drained, hardly more than a croak. And now he tried to raise his hand to point a quivering finger over Leila's shoulder.

"It's all right, Mark, Hitchman's back to normal, he – "

Mark shook his head and tried to stand. Leila started to ease him back, meanwhile glancing behind herself to see that Hitchman was indeed in no further danger. And then she saw what Mark had been trying to warn her about…not Hitchman, but the appearance of the huge fiber-optic cable. It had by now reached the roof, broken through, and was weaving in the air close to the transmission tower. Its intention was obvious – it was going to connect itself to the tower so that the evil force that had already possessed so many people would be broadcast across the city.

And if that happened, the entire population would be turned into TV zombies.

Mark's weakened hand touched Leila's arm. "Fire…fire…," he croaked feebly.

"No, Mark, fire won't stop it!"

Mark shook his head again. "Fire…h-hose…"

Understanding blazed through her. She glanced around and saw the fire reel bracketed to the wall close by. Leaving Mark, Leila ran across and, by the uncertain glimmer of the lightning flashes, read the operating instructions. They seemed simple enough, although whether the plan would work was another question entirely.

It took all of the strength in her right arm to haul the thick fire hose out onto the roof - but she still needed to release her sprained arm from its sling to clamp the hose against her body while, with her other hand, she slipped the safety bolt free and twisted the nozzle.

The pressure of water that blasted from the

hose lifted Leila off her feet and threw her into the air. Luckily, she kept the presence of mind to hang on, though the hose whipped her across the roof and sent her skimming toward the edge. It loomed closer – ten feet – six – three – until Leila found herself looking over the low parapet wall, at the tiny moving lights of the traffic below, almost lost in the densely falling sheets of rain.

Mark had known the water pressure would take Leila by surprise, but she had dashed away before he could warn her. Now, as he saw her danger, Mark dragged himself onto hands and knees and crawled to take hold of the hose.

He used it like a support, helping him to stand and brace his weight against the power of the water within. He could feel it pulsing like living muscle, gallons of water jetting through every second. He leaned back, hauling on the hose, pulling Leila away from the edge.

She caught sight of him and beamed with relief. Then together, as Mark dragged himself closer to her, they heaved the hose around to point toward the tower.

The cable had reared itself twenty feet or more into the air, the end of it alive with brilliant, crackling sparks. It wove this way and that like a snake, as though searching for a point of connection. Then it struck, forcing itself into what looked like the main junction box.

In that second, with an immense and final effort, Mark and Leila brought the water jet to bear. The geyser smashed into the cable. For a single terrible second, nothing happened – then the sky cracked apart with blue sheet-flame and hurled the cable away, the backsurge of energy shattering it into a million diamond splinters.

Mark and Leila dropped to the ground as the hurricane of fragments blew over. When they dared to look up, what remained lay like melted, blackened plastic at the base of the tower. White smoke, bitter with the stink of burning, wafted by...and across the sky a thousand ghosts of unknown movie stars wailed and scattered among the clouds.

Chapter 17

When Roy eventually checked the roof for his friends, he found Mark and Leila sitting together by the power house. They were laughing uncontrollably, while the fire hose sprayed a great fan of water over the edge of the building.

"Well," he said in pleasure and surprise, "well, it looks like you've been through the wars!"

"You, too." Leila jabbed a finger to point out Roy's black eye and swollen cheek, before collapsing into helpless laughter once more.

And Roy grinned with them, sharing their joy at being alive. What they had done was foolish, yet brave. And though they might not know it, the two kids had saved the staff of Solid Broadcast and, by the looks of it, most of the people of Kenniston. They deserved their moment of triumph…

Before the final battle began.

☠

Roy shut off the fire hose. Then he and Mark hauled Andy Hitchman to his feet and helped him back down the stairs to the control room.

"It looks like a bomb's hit it!" Leila exclaimed as she followed them through. Furniture lay smashed and overturned; TV screens had been broken; sheets of paper were scattered everywhere. About thirty people were inside the room, some of them on the floor, looking dazed, others helping to tend the cuts and scrapes of their friends and co-workers. Leila scanned faces, sighing with relief to see that all of them were human.

"It was a close thing," Roy commented. "I should have realized earlier that SBTV would be a prime target."

They heard many footsteps clattering on the stairs, and a moment later Sergeant Holmes burst in, followed by a dozen police officers. He paused in surprise, pushing back his peaked cap to scratch his forehead wryly.

"What's been going on here, Roy? It looks like a bomb's hit the place!"

Roy, Mark, and Leila grinned at each other.

"Um, it's a long story. Look, Tony, we'll explain what's happened. And even if it sounds incredible, I'm begging you to believe us. After that, I'll need as many officers as you can spare for a raid on Zoffany's – "

Holmes held up his hands. "Wait a minute, Roy. Before you go any further, I don't *have* any officers to spare right now. Almost the entire force is busy checking out missing-persons reports. And then there's the business of this freak weather: we've had flood warnings, power cuts, electrical fires…"

"That's my point," Roy replied. "All of this is being caused by Zoffany. The very heart of what's happening lies somewhere inside the MZTV studios. Zoffany tried to take over the population of Kenniston in one go by attacking this building. He failed – thanks to these two rebels here. But

106

now that he *has* failed, he'll try all the harder to spread his influence across the city."

Roy went on to explain about the way the fiber-optic cables had been "growing" through the ground, outward from Zoffany's studios; and that how, once they reached a television set, they were able to control whoever watched it.

"Like hypnotism, you mean?" Holmes suggested. Roy shrugged.

"I don't think so, Tony. I think this is something else completely."

"But it's even worse than Roy says," Leila broke in. "The cable doesn't have to plug into a TV – it can plug straight into a person!"

"She's right," Roy agreed. He described their encounter with Torrance.

"Some terrible, dark power is trying to cast its shadow over humanity. How it started, and why it started at MZTV, remains a mystery. But unless we do something about it, and do something now, I don't think we'll stand a chance."

Holmes recognized the seriousness in Roy's face. He took a deep breath, then gave a long, shuddering sigh.

"Roy, I'll speak plainly. It all sounds like mumbo-jumbo to me. But *something* strange is obviously going on. I've trusted your word on things for years – and I'm going to trust it now. However, the chief will need further evidence before he releases more men to my command. Give me until tomorrow, and I'll see what I can do. Okay?"

"Thanks, Tony, I'm grateful."

The two men shook hands, though Roy couldn't help thinking, "If tomorrow isn't too late…"

☠

They drove home in the aftermath of the storm. As they had seen from the roof of SBTV, the deluge had been very local: just the studio building itself and a few blocks around it. Once they were clear of Kenniston center, the clouds thinned to a fine, high veil, and the sun shone down warmly. It was a beautiful autumn afternoon.

"It must be something to do with the huge energy build up," Mark suggested.

"The static electricity in the air."

Roy nodded in agreement. "Whatever's mounting this invasion is generating vast amounts of power – enough to create a brand new building out of crumbled bricks and rusted iron girders." He explained what he and Mark had seen in the empty lot behind MZTV. "And strong enough to take over people's minds and transform them into blind puppets."

"But why do you suppose the *Shadow*," Leila said, deliberately using the word that had first sprung into her mind, "is bothering to take over people using television screens? Why doesn't it get directly into their heads?"

"Everyone watches TV," Roy replied. "And while you do, you feel safe. Also, whole families and groups of friends might be gazing at a single screen. And so, more people can be 'captured' more easily that way."

Mark frowned. "What about the people who've disappeared, like...," his voice quavered, "like Tina and Gary?"

"That's something different, I would say." Roy paused at a junction, then sped across and turned into the parking lot of his apartment building. "I think the ones who have disappeared completely, and not just changed, have been taken for some other purpose, a special purpose."

"But what?"

"That," he said, "is what I aim to find out."

Climbing out of the car, Roy, Leila, and Mark walked toward the front entrance of the apartment building. Once inside, they were puzzled to see the elevator doors opening and closing sporadically – until Leila spotted a cobweb of electrical filaments dancing over the control box in the wall nearby.

"No...," she whispered as the blood drained from her face. "Oh no, not them, too..."

Together the three sped up the stairs, slammed open the fire door at the end of the corridor, then ran madly for Roy's apartment.

They found the door open and the apartment quite empty. Leila's parents, and Sarah Watkins, had vanished without a trace of how, or why. Except for the MZTV logo – the phoenix in the flames – that had been burned into the glass of the television screen.

Chapter 18

Roy could understand why his young friends raged and shouted, could see quite clearly why they wanted to grab any weapon they could find and go storming into the MZTV studios. They were filled with anger and hurt, and they wanted revenge.

He put up with it for ten minutes, then stood and yelled, "Enough!"

Mark and Leila, red-faced and bright-eyed in their fury, stopped in mid sentence and glared at him.

"This isn't helping," he said more quietly, and with infinite patience now. "It's not helping you, or me, your families, or any of the other people who've been taken into Zoffany's domain. If we rush blindly in, then we won't stand a chance. Zoffany will be waiting...and behind Zoffany, the Shadow."

Mark shivered, as though someone had walked over his grave. "What do you think the Shadow is?" he asked in a small voice.

Roy considered this for a moment, his gaze moving beyond them to the window and the distant horizon. "Something very ancient, something filled with bitterness and hate: a figure that hangs like a mist in the background when there's violence, or war, or unhappiness. Its heart is twisted. It despises a laughing child or two young people in love. It hides from the sunshine. It loathes and fears courage and hope – which is why, Mark, Leila, we need to have both in the days to come."

The tone of Roy's voice had changed. It was almost as though he were speaking to himself alone, lost in a past he had half-forgotten. Leila and Mark glanced at one another, then Leila went over and touched Roy's hand.

"How do you know all of this?" she wondered softly.

"I'm older than you, I've seen more. My work has taken me to some dark and terrible places. I've glimpsed the Shadow moving there behind things. I've seen its face…"

"What does it look like, Roy?" Mark was thinking of the Reptiloids and other monstrous creatures from his game of *Mutant Wars*. Would it have purple skin, or green, and would its mouth be black or red inside – and with how many daggerlike teeth?

Roy Case smiled at the boy, pleased that he was still just that: at least he, and Leila too, had not been tainted by the Shadow's bitter-cold touch.

He shrugged. "It has many shapes; a crying baby, an old woman who seems to be lost…a handsome young man in a suit, or the most beautiful girl you ever saw. But that's its 'outside face': within, it is so distorted that you may not even recognize it."

"And is it just called 'the Shadow'?" Leila asked.

"It has a thousand names, some of which I guess we have never discovered – "

"What name do you give it, Roy?"

Roy regarded the boy frankly, before looking

away. He spoke as if in pain.

"In the night, in the dark, when I wake from a nightmare that haunts me even though my eyes are open – I know the Shadow has passed over. And at such times, I call it Despair…"

☠

"I've got it!" Mark leaped from his chair as his voice bounced and echoed around the high ceiling of Kenniston Public Library. Several people snapped annoyed glances at him; one middle-aged woman in tweeds said, "Ssshhh!"

Mark apologized with a look and hurried over to where Leila and Roy were scanning bound volumes of old newspapers, books, and archive material on a microfiche machine. He laid an ancient copy of *Who's Who* in front of his friends, tapping the page with his forefinger.

"Well done." Roy smiled up at him, then studied the book and began to read:

"'Maxwell Curtis Zoffany, born in Arkham, New England, November 1st, 1885. Best known as a producer and director of romantic films, some with an historical perspective…blah blah blah…Reached his peak in the late Thirties with titles such as 'Forever Yours,' 'The Black Velvet Necklace,' and 'Bitter Pearls'…blah blah…His small film company, Phoenix Productions, based in the city of Kenniston, created over eighty films between 1929 and the early 1940s, when the Second World War and the changing tastes of the movie-going public contributed to the studio's decline."

"Although Zoffany oversaw the making of another dozen pictures between 1940 and 1942, these were seen as increasingly dated, and none of them showed a profit at the box office. In its final year, Phoenix Productions ran up several large debts. Staff were laid off and a number of the studio's star names walked out. The final blow came in the autumn of 1943 when, on a cold November night, a fire swept through the building. No definite cause was ever uncovered, although some commentators at the time felt that Zoffany had set the fire himself to claim on the studio's insurance policies."

"Most likely, the true explanation will never be known – for although no bodies were recovered from the blaze, it is almost certain that Maxwell Zoffany remained inside the studio he had loved for so long, as a captain might remain with his doomed and sinking ship…"

Roy's voice trailed into silence. Mark wiped self-consciously at his moistening eyes.

"Poor man," Leila said. "He tried so hard. He made all those pictures with happy endings, but his own story was so terribly sad."

"Wait a minute." Mark held up a hand. "If Zoffany was born in 1885, that would make him over 110 years old today – even if he did survive the fire, which is doubtful."

"Remember the phoenix," Roy answered darkly. "The mythical bird that rose anew from the ashes of its own destruction. Zoffany did just that. And not just the man, but his entire production company – rising straight out of the ground and into the twenty-first century!"

"But you can't do that!" Mark protested.

"You can if you have help…"

"Help? Who could give you that kind of help?"

"The one," Leila said, understanding at last, "who is always ready to strike a bargain…"

While Mark and Roy went to ask permission to copy the article on Zoffany, Leila read through it again, then looked at the picture of the man himself on the next page. He was rather plump-faced and balding, with a wan smile and a face that was lined with more than just age. The picture must have been taken close to the end of Zoffany's life, Leila guessed. It was a good picture, too, showing him in a natural pose, with posters of some of his films on the wall behind him.

Leila touched the image, and in that moment forgave Max Zoffany his trespasses. Because she had just noticed his eyes and what lay beyond them: the worst thing she could ever imagine.

Despair.

Chapter 19

Roy made some phone calls as soon as they returned to his apartment. He spoke first with Sergeant Holmes – not at the station, but at the cop's home number, since he was off duty. Holmes said that, since he'd last seen Roy, he'd had a change of mind. People seemed to be vanishing in the hundreds now: the precinct switchboard was jammed with calls and reports.

"We're working in shifts," Holmes went on, "eight hours on, eight hours off. It's mayhem down there."

"What made you believe our story, Tony?" Roy wondered casually.

Down the line, Holmes laughed rather sheepishly. "You're going to think *I'm* crazy this time – but I'm watching MZTV right now, and the people in the films and commercials, well, they look just like some of the missing-persons photographs we've received. In fact, there's one guy on now who – "

Roy interrupted him, speaking urgently down the phone. "Tony – you mean you're *watching* MZTV, now?"

"Sure I am. I don't think much of the new stuff, but these old movies are – "

"Tony, switch off the television set! Switch it off and get out of there at once!"

"Hey, keep cool, Roy, I'm only…aw, now the picture's gone funny. Wait a moment, let me…"

"Tony – Tony listen to me – *Get out of there, now!*"

Over the phone line, Roy heard his friend put the receiver down on the table. There was also, in the background, the hissing, crackling sound that he knew all too well…and then Holmes swearing at the TV set as he evidently attempted to fiddle with the controls.

"Tony!" Roy bellowed in a final, futile warning.

Holmes's voice broke over the telephone: "Hey, now that's *really* weird…the picture seems to be coming out of…the light, it's…no – no – *agghhh!* The light!"

Something swept by the telephone with the sound of waves crashing against cliffs. There was a clatter of plastic, a sudden series of loud cracklings. Then silence.

Roy replaced the receiver. His face was grim.

"They took Sergeant Holmes, too?" Leila said. "Oh, Roy, I'm sorry…"

"All the more reason to get over to Hob's Lane and MZTV quickly." He pointed. "Through there, in my study, you'll find a baseball bat, a ceremonial sword I bought in Japan, and a Kukri knife from India. Bring them, would you? Meanwhile, I need to make another call – one that just might make all the difference…"

☠

The afternoon was waning as the three sped across town in Roy's rented car. The worst of the rush hour traffic was over, and so they made good time in reaching the southern side of Kenniston, and from there the old rundown industrial quarter.

Even so, the sky was darkening and shadows reached out across the deserted streets by the time they swung into Hob's Lane and pulled up under a streetlight.

They climbed out of the car. Roy carried his huge, deadly looking sword; Mark wielded the baseball bat; Leila nervously clutched the curved knife in her right hand. They stood together, looking down the street at the brash façade of the MZTV building.

The gathering night seemed full of menace.

"What are we waiting for?" Mark asked. His nerves felt raw with this inaction. Despite the danger, he much preferred the thought of going straight in to face whatever he needed to face; to fight whatever battles were necessary to save his friends and loved ones.

"We are waiting – " Roy replied a moment later, " – for that!"

He put his hand to his ear – but now the sound could be plainly heard; the wailing howl of sirens echoing in the distance. There came the faint screech of brakes – and again, much louder, behind them.

A patrol car swerved around the corner, its rear end sliding. High-beam headlights blazed across the trio. The car stopped. Someone stepped out.

"It's not the cavalry," Officer Connor said, rather jauntily. "But I'm better than nothing…"

Roy grinned and shook the young officer by the hand. "We need all the help we can get."

The cop's face grew serious. "When you told me what happened to the Sarge, I figured I had to do something. Oh, by the way, I made a couple of phone calls myself – I hope you don't mind, but I think the team I contacted might prove useful."

"Who?" Roy asked.

"Only the fire department," Connor said, laughing.

☠

The four of them approached the studio in the patrol car, slowly. "Looks like everyone's gone home," Connor commented. Roy shook his head.

"Oh no, they're all there, somewhere inside; all the people we've come to save, and the ones who are beyond saving…"

The young cop stared at Roy in puzzlement, but he would say no more.

Connor trickled the car to a halt, but kept the engine idling and the lights on high.

"Maybe the fire crews have been delayed," he said. "There could have been an emergency somewhere. What shall we do?"

"I don't think we can afford to wait much longer. The more people Zoffany captures, the more his influence grows."

And the darker the Shadow becomes, Leila added mentally.

"Let's do it then!" Mark pushed open the door and stepped out. The others followed.

They stood in front of the headlights, feeling reassured by their brilliance. Overhead, the deep blue of the evening sky was giving way to the duller, dirtier grey of clouds swirling in with dramatic speed from all directions. Roy knew that the clouds would continue to thicken, deepen, until they were ripe enough to bear rain and lightning. For this was the power of the Shadow here, now, in this world of modern technology. Raw electricity could smash down buildings or drive the most delicate machinery. And it was massing above them, a million times more potent than knives and swords or any human weapon.

From far away came the faint crack and roll of thunder.

"Come on," Roy said, and led them forward to the main doors of the MZTV building.

Ten yards out, they stopped, for the doors were opening…and now a man stepped through to meet them – or something that had once been a man.

It was wearing the remnants of a dark suit, but the cloth was rotten and crumbling. The man's hair looked like black string, coarsely combed; its ears were flaps of wrinkled leather.

It turned, holding out a bony hand as a second figure stepped over the studio threshold. This time, a woman wearing a dress that looked as though it had been buried for a long, long time. The papery skin around her mouth crinkled into the mockery of a smile. Their hands interlocked with a rattle of fingerbones.

"Sylvia," the man said in a creaky, halting voice, *"I love you so much…I will always love you - until the end of time."*

"*Oh Gordon,*" sighed the lady, looking up adoringly into the dusty black sockets of his eyes, *"you mean so much to me!"*

They kissed, and Gordon's jaw swung wide,

clunking against his collarbone, while Sylvia's skull flopped sideways onto her shoulder.

Leila screamed in fear and pity and loss –

Then there came a sound from behind them, as somebody turned out the headlights.

Chapter 20

Because of the dim streetlights and the looming black clouds, Roy and the others could see only vague shapes gathering around the patrol car. Even so, there was no doubt about what the figures were – people from the past: ghosts, lonely wandering souls, trapped here by Zoffany's broken dream.

One or two of them began to moan; a few started to cry. Caught by the breeze as the wind direction changed, their scraps of moldering dresses and suits flapped and swished about them. And that same breeze carried with it a smell – a smell of dry bones and earth and dust.

"These are the ones who believed Zoffany's promises," Leila said quietly. There was deep sorrow in her voice.

"Not Zoffany," Roy corrected, "but the *Shadow's* promises. My guess is that Zoffany was fooled, just like all of these poor folks."

"Poor folks!" Connor laughed uneasily. "Just look at them, Roy…they're out to get us!"

Roy was shaking his head. "They're still living in the past, dreaming the same old dream of stardom. They've been sent to delay us, that's all."

"Delay us?" Mark frowned. "Why only delay us…?"

No sooner was the question asked than the answer came into view.

Beyond the chainlink fence of the wasteland, a light was swiftly growing. And together with the light, a hissing, a crackling of mounting energy. Hands like glowing light bulbs grabbed at the fence; dozens of fizzing, shining bodies pressed against it. The support posts began to sag and the metal links started breaking with a sharp clinking sound.

The fence gave way in several places, and the creatures of light streamed through.

As they came, they chanted: "*MZTV – MZTV – it's the only one for me!*"

Roy, Connor, Leila, and Mark began to back off, step by step, toward the entrance to the studios.

The creatures poured into the street and came on like a chaotic wave of brilliance. The chanting grew louder, swelling into a deafening thunder –

"*MZTV – MZTV – It's the only one for me!*"

"Stop it!" Leila screamed, clamping her hands to her ears and cowering away. She turned to run – and found herself staring into Gordon's melted face. Things were crawling over it, as though a stone had just been lifted away. He grinned at her.

"*Darling – kiss me now, my sweet…*"

Leila's screaming reached a new pitch. Roy, seeing what was happening, threw himself toward the figure and pushed it away. Gordon went stumbling into the night, meaningless words bubbling from his dried-out lips.

As Roy held Leila to calm her, two fire engines roared around the corner of Hob's Lane. Connor gave a whoop of joy. He had spoken to the fire chief earlier, and the crews knew what to expect.

The fire trucks screeched to a halt, coming alongside the advancing creatures of light. Men in thick, protective oilskins and yellow hard hats jumped out. Within seconds they had unreeled their hoses.

At the chief's word of command, the jets were turned on with a bang. One sprayed directly over the oncoming crowd; the other was aimed higher, to send a ceaseless rain beyond the fence into the wasteland. Sparks snapped and popped around the teeming, writhing creatures; blue lightning ran like liquid fire over their bodies; the chanting dissolved into a mass of shrieks and howls.

One of the creatures blinked out – and a very ordinary-looking man slumped to the ground with a groan.

"He'll be sorry he watched MZTV when he wakes up!" the fire chief grinned.

The same thing was happening to other people now. The blue electrical energy was shorting out, and men and women were becoming normal again.

"There's a third hose we haven't used yet," the chief told Roy cheerfully. "Any ideas?"

"Can your men cope out here?" Roy asked. The chief nodded confidently.

"Fine. Then unreel the hose as far as you can – because we're going in there…"

He pointed through the darkened front doorway of the MZTV building.

There was a brief argument as Roy tried to persuade Leila and Mark to stay outside in safety. He soon learned how stubborn and determined teenagers can be.

"Do you really think," Leila said, hands on hips, "that we'd come this far, and then chicken out of the grand finale?"

"But – " Roy tried to say.

"Our parents are in there, and Tina."

"But – "

"And Gary," Leila added.

"And anyway," Mark said with finality, "this is much more exciting than *Mutant Wars* any day!"

Roy's shoulders slumped. He gave a sigh of defeat.

"Okay, okay, you win. But let's hurry. If the Shadow sees his army being beaten, it might do something *really* serious!"

It was decided that the fire chief would remain outside the studio building and direct operations from the street. A fireman showed Officer Connor how to operate the hose nozzle. Roy led the way, with Connor at his side and Mark and Leila just a pace behind.

The four paused at the threshold, casting a last look at the bright red fire trucks, the crews busily spraying geysers of water at the crowd, the sprawled forms of people changed back to their normal selves...

Then they swung around and stepped through into the unknown.

124

Chapter 21

Doors crashed open and from all sides more creatures of light swept through.

Connor yelled in alarm and began fumbling with the jet control. Roy whipped his sword around in a twinkling arc and slashed at one of the beings. But a snake of electricity flashed down the blade and drove needles of fiery pain into his hand and arm. He cried out in shock as the sword went spinning away, to land in a clatter out of reach, the hot steel smoking.

Fortunately, Connor got the hose working and the jet exploded outward in a fierce gush. Nearby creatures were blasted aside. Others, further away, wilted and collapsed under the ceaseless drenching. The air filled with steam and hissings, stray sparks that spurted like shooting stars, flames like vapor that quickly died away to nothing, so that gradually the brilliance faded and the moment of panic passed.

"So much light," muttered Leila, rubbing at her eyes. Roy put his arm around her shoulder.

"Where the light is brightest, the darkest shadows are cast."

"That sounds like a wise old proverb."

He smiled at her. "Actually, I just made it up as I went along."

"Look there!" Mark's excited exclamation startled them all. "It's Mr. and Mrs. Carpenter."

He rushed over to check that the old couple were unharmed. Leila looked around her. "And that's the Sweet family: they live opposite us…"

"Obviously," Roy explained, "the Shadow's power is not unbreakable this time."

Leila frowned at him. "This time?"

"The Shadow has chosen electricity as its weapon on this occasion – electricity used to create television pictures, or in its raw form to control the people it captured. But electricity can be defeated by water…the Shadow will learn that now, so that when it comes the next time, it will be prepared."

Connor shut off the water jet with a snap. Apart from the gentle music of dripping, a deep silence closed in around them all.

"Let's move on," Roy said, offering no further explanation.

Nor did Mark or Leila feel comfortable in asking him for one.

☠

They made their way through a doorway at random and came to a long corridor that seemed to stretch on forever. Other doors led off to the left and right as far as they could see.

"Which way?" Mark asked. Roy pointed.

"Left. Always left, in the Shadow's domain."

"Um, Roy, this hose won't reach any further…" Connor gave it a tug.

"Then leave it there," Roy said, and turned away. Leila noticed he seemed more serious now, as though, after so many struggles had been won, the last great crisis still lay ahead.

Roy slammed the first door on the left wide

open, and his companions followed him through.

They found themselves moving through an old film studio; one that looked as though it hadn't been used for many, many years. Above them, the ceiling was lost in the darkness. But huge, rusting spotlights hung down on thick wires, or gazed from the ends of long metal booms like strangely angled eyes. Tall drapes and curtains of decaying cloth were pulled across here and there: hanging fragments resembling bats's wings or – Mark gulped – the smelly cloaks of hungry vampires. Big, boxy film cameras stood on their wheeled dollies, while scattered all over the floor lay scraps of old movie film. Leila picked one up and squinted at faces of people she didn't know, before dropping it at her feet.

"It's like stepping back into the past," Connor commented. Roy nodded.

"Either that, or else the old studio has come back to haunt us!"

"Don't talk like that," Leila pleaded. "It scares me."

"We're all scared, honey," Connor told her. "Even a big, strong, handsome guy like me. Why, I'm quaking in my boots."

She smiled at him. Mark said, "Don't worry, officer, I'm here to protect you."

They began walking across the ancient film set, their feet crunching over forgotten celluloid. Faded backdrops, with paint peeling, showed seascapes and woods, fine old houses, splendid gardens – all of it hung with veils of dusty cobwebs.

Then somewhere far away, they heard a voice

calling, and footsteps tapping across the worm-eaten wooden floorboards. The group froze. A door creaked open – and closed – the footsteps grew louder.

A faint breeze stirred the cobweb swathes and crinkled the scraps of film like autumn leaves. A heavy curtain swung lazily. Mark wrinkled his nose as dry dust drifted past his face.

Without any warning, one of the spotlights at head height sizzled on. For a moment the group was dazzled by it. But then a figure stepped in front of the beam and came striding toward them.

"*You're out of bounds, you know,*" said a polite young female voice. Officer Connor reached out and pushed the spotlight aside. And now they could see the girl's smiling face, which Leila recognized as the face of one the tour guides who had first shown them round.

"I thought MZTV welcomed visitors," Roy replied, his body tense and ready to move.

"*Only during the day, I'm afraid. At night –*"

"But surely more interesting things happen here at night."

"Besides," Leila added cheekily, "we hate crowds of sightseers."

The tour guide's smile dropped away. She glared at Leila with hostile eyes. And Leila once again found herself revolted by the woman's over-thick makeup: it was like the heavy makeup old film actors used to wear years and years ago.

"*I said, the studio is closed. You'll have to leave…*"

She moved forward and took Leila firmly by the shoulders.

"Let go of me!" Leila shrugged the woman's arms away. One hand came up and slapped Leila sharply across the face. In her temper, Leila struck out with her nails, raking away the white, crusty makeup of the tour guide's face – and revealing yellow bone beneath.

The tour guide roared, and her mouth was as black as a cave inside. She clenched a fist to strike Leila down.

"You leave my girl alone!" Mark had been carrying his baseball bat all this time. Now he gripped it in both hands, swung it high and crashed it around into the tour guide's stomach.

The woman doubled over and staggered back, crashing into a tall scenery flat, which toppled and smashed down on top of her, whooshing up clouds of choking gray dust.

"Let's get out of here," Connor suggested.

They hurried toward the far exit.

"Hey, Mark," Leila said tentatively as they walked, "I didn't know I was your girl…"

He blushed instantly, a deep red, and struggled for words. "Um – er – well – that is…would you like to be? Please?"

"Sure." Leila flicked back her hair. "As long as you promise *never* to take me to the movies!"

Roy interrupted them. "Let me go through this door first, just to make sure – "

He never finished the sentence.

Without warning a deep, rumbling sound filled the air. They all turned in time to see one of the heavy cameras bearing quickly down upon them, ready to crush them to death against the wall.

Chapter 22

Connor shoved Leila roughly aside; Mark leaped clear himself. Roy looked over his shoulder at the speeding camera, then kicked open the door in front of him. They all watched as the big machine trundled through, disappearing along a dark passage into a dim distance.

They followed it cautiously, Connor unsnapping a flashlight from its clip on his belt. When he turned the flashlight on, there was no sign of the camera, just the passageway fading into shadows.

"Where the heck are we now?" Mark wanted to know.

Connor gave a chuckle. "I've no idea - but I think I'd rather be tucked in bed at home!"

Roy was having his doubts about going farther down the passage. He was well aware that they were moving deeper into the Shadow's territory, walking more surely into what was probably a trap. Now they could all hear faraway bangings and hammering sounds, as though people were trying to break through windows, doors, and perhaps even the walls.

"That'll be the guys from the fire department," Connor judged. "I guess they decided it was time to get us out!"

Leila looked horrified. "But we haven't found Gary yet, or Tina and the others!"

"Yes, we have," Mark said quietly. He had walked a few yards ahead of his friends, and was now gazing through a circular porthole

130

window, his face illuminated by a pale white fluttering light.

Frowning, the others gathered around to see what Mark had discovered.

It was a movie theater, packed with hundreds of people. They were sitting absolutely still, their unblinking eyes gazing unwaveringly at the screen. An old black and white film was playing; and through the swing doorway to the cinema, the group could hear the muffled sounds of dialogue, which sounded to Mark as corny as the scene he'd witnessed earlier.

"Why…" Leila swallowed hard, guessing the answer to the question on her lips.

"Why don't they get up and leave?"

"They can't," Roy said flatly. "This must be part of the bargain Zoffany made: to see his movie theater full again. These people are trapped there – trapped for all eternity; forced to watch the same old films again and again and again."

"Unless we do something about it!" The look on Connor's face was fierce.

Roy nodded once, with determination.

"Unless we do something about it…Mark, Leila – I have a hunch that if we can stop that film, the spell will be broken and the audience will return to normal. Would you stay here and help Officer Connor to guide the people to safety?"

"What about you?"

"I'm going to find the projection room, Leila," Roy said. "And destroy it."

The search was brief. After turning left along

the passage, Roy came to the blank gray door of the projection room. His sword had been left behind in the lobby, but he'd borrowed Mark's baseball bat and Connor's flashlight to help him in his task.

He went inside.

In the gloom, Roy could see the projector throwing its bright beam through the glass window into the auditorium, the machine rattling softly as the film was drawn through. The rest of the room was in darkness, but even so, Roy could make out a hunched figure sitting behind the projector, leaning forward as though engrossed in the movie.

Roy clicked on the flashlight, and gasped.

The projectionist had been dead a long time. He was no more than a skeleton dressed in a shirt draped loosely over the bones. A crumbling cap sat at an angle on his skull. One bony hand, curled to a fist, propped up his chin as he stared sightlessly along the projection beam. His white smile stretched almost from ear to ear.

Roy took a deep breath to calm himself down. He walked over to the big black projector and scanned it for a control switch. Spotting one, he reached down to flick it to the "Off" position.

A skeleton hand fell over Roy's hand, and squeezed.

The skull head turned toward him.

"Can't do that, sir," said an echoing voice from deep underground. *"Can't have you doing that now, can we?"*

The projectionist's hands reached for Roy's throat.

Roy groaned, pushed the skeleton's arms away, and jammed the flashlight solidly into its open mouth.

The flashlight stayed on and the skull glowed amber yellow like a Halloween lamp. But still it came, rising from its chair, arms reaching again for Roy's face, for his eyes…

Roy stumbled backward, kicking aside metal film cannisters, boxes, and a small table. Sweat was dripping from his face and his heart was hammering furiously.

The skeleton lurched closer, like a jerky puppet, its face aglow in the flashlight.

Roy drew back his bat, aimed, and swung it with all his strength at the hideous yellow head.

The skull exploded like a china vase, sending fragments tinkling all across the room; the flashlight went spinning away and was lost. The projectionist's body collapsed with a clackety-clack of loose bones. But the hands were still active, scuttling across the floor like great spiders to tug at the hem of Roy's pants.

Kicking one away and stamping on the other with his heel, he lifted the baseball bat again and, with a bellow of desperation, smashed it down on the back of the ghostly film projector.

Chapter 23

In the auditorium, the film on the huge screen suddenly went haywire, the faces of the actors sliding grotesquely sideways, dissolving into chaos. The bright white beam of the projector continued to blaze outward for a few moments, but then it, too, died, and the theater was plunged into darkness.

Mark, Leila, and Connor had already pushed through the doors and gone inside. They froze as the blackness engulfed them – gulping with relief as dim red emergency lights came on.

A stirring began to fill the great room, a rustling and shuffling as the audience started waking. One or two voices called out in confusion and fear above the growing hubbub. Officer Connor clambered up onto the stage below the screen, his body cast in silhouette against the screen's soft red glow.

"Ladies and gentlemen – listen to me, please! My name is Martin Connor and I'm a police officer. I know you feel rather dazed at this moment, and probably have a thousand questions to ask! All of them will be answered later…For now, will you please leave the theater in an orderly manner. Go out through that door and – um – then…"

"Turn right!" Leila shouted. "Always right!"

Connor smiled in gratitude and nodded to show that he had heard. "Turn right, ladies and gentlemen, keep turning right until you reach the outside! Go now! Go now!"

The crowd began to move sluggishly toward the one exit. Connor jumped down and pushed through the aisle to help. Roy appeared from the corridor side and eased his way through the press of the crowd.

"I'll lead them to safety," Connor said. "And get the chief to send in some reinforcements!"

"Okay." Roy nodded, searching for Mark and Leila. He caught sight of them a second or two later. They were hugging their parents, Gary, and Tina, tears of joy running down their faces.

Roy smiled as he approached them.

"What's going on?" Gary was asking. Tina's eyes lit up as she recognized Roy.

"Oh, Mr. Case...oh, I...wow – can I have your autograph please?"

"Not now, Tina," Mark tutted impatiently. "Just get out of here and we'll talk later."

The girl's face tightened with irritation. "Now just wait a moment, you little..." she began. Mark gave her one last hug and a big, wet kiss on the cheek.

"I love you, Sis. See you outside..."

Shaking her head, Tina did as she was told.

The crowd was thinning now as more and more of them streamed through the doorway. Roy glanced around, checking for anyone left in their seats. "Another couple of minutes and we should be clear."

"Roy – " Leila tugged at his sleeve. "Look at the screen."

They looked. The screen had become *redder*,

somehow, and yet darker, too. And caught on it like a moth trapped behind a lampshade, the figure of a man was struggling to be free.

Roy hurried forward and leaped up onto the stage, Mark and Leila following closely behind.

By the time they reached the spot, the fabric of the screen was bulging outward, and incredibly, the rather plump body of the man was oozing through, to drop with a thump to the floor.

"It's Max Zoffany," Leila said quietly, recognizing him from his photograph at the library.

"He doesn't look so tough!" Mark sneered. Roy and Leila knelt beside him.

Zoffany opened his eyes and gave a gurgling, strangled gasp, as though he'd been drowning.

"You…" His face squeezed up in a spasm of coughing. "You – freed – me…He didn't keep – his promise!" Anger hardened his voice, but sorrow, an instant later, softened it once more. "I only wanted to entertain people…make them sad, sometimes – but make their hearts glad in the end…everyone finds joy in love…"

"We stopped the projector, Zoffany," Roy explained. "We broke the bargain – and so you have a second chance. Do you understand that? You can decide all over again what is the best thing to do."

Zoffany's features twisted in deep regret. "I had my day…but I wanted it to go on forever! I wanted the crowds to love my pictures for all time! What a fool I was."

He glanced at the faces of the rather stern-looking man and the pretty girl and the boy beyond them. "I'm sorry," he whispered, "for all the harm I have caused. I'm sorry. And I *have* decided now, what the best thing is to do. The bargain is ended. My day – is – done…"

"Mr. Zoffany…" Leila stooped very near to him, for his eyes were closing and his grip on her hand was growing weaker. "I'd love to see your movies…I'll find them and watch them."

The pudgy fingers squeezed her hand briefly, then relaxed.

"And, Mr. Zoffany, we forgive you…"

His hand flopped loosely to his side. Zoffany's slow, shallow breathing ceased entirely.

"Leave him now," Roy whispered, easing Leila away. "It's time we were off…"

"It certainly is," Mark said, his voice rising in alarm. He pointed a trembling finger at the huge movie screen.

It was *much* redder now, and a dry, painful heat was radiating from it. Patches of brown scorching were appearing here and there. And behind the screen, something was swiftly approaching.

Something vast.

Something unbelievable.

"Out! Now!"

Roy lost no time in being polite. He almost threw the two teenagers off the stage and hurried them toward the exit. Bustling them through the swing door, he turned briefly to check behind.

The screen burst into flames and a nightmare

plowed through, filling the auditorium with the stink of burning and a deafening roar of pure fury.

The three ran as they had never run before, caring nothing for the pain in their muscles or the agony of their lungs dragging in great gulps of air.

Behind them, waves of heat seared the walls: and there came a series of mighty detonations as bricks were crushed to powder; broad, wooden beams were snapped and splintered like matchsticks; metal girders were twisted and pulled apart like licorice – the whole building being torn asunder.

"It's destroying the theater!" Roy yelled, snatching at Mark as he turned around a corner. "Not that way – follow Leila. Go right, always go right!"

They ran at full speed through the decaying film set, which was falling and disintegrating around them, along stifling, smoky passageways toward the lobby.

Up ahead, they could see the doors that led to the outside and freedom.

Leila got there first, slamming through them and racing across the lobby.

Mark was three paces behind. He was about to follow when he heard a shout of dismay behind him and the heavy thump of Roy tripping and falling to the floor.

He stopped and turned to help...and his heart went cold.

Looking beyond Roy, Mark could see the Shadow storming along the corridor with the speed and power of an express train. Only now, it was not a shadow – but a thing with a hundred thrashing limbs, a thousand serpent eyes, glassy with hate; jaws the size of a room, lined with teeth that were bigger than swords...and a hideous body, swathed in flame, that looked as though nothing could ever stop it.

Mark almost passed out with terror. But Roy had stunned himself in falling and lay helplessly in the path of the leviathan: so Mark knew he had no choice but to stay and help his friend...

He had noticed the fire hose that Connor had discarded earlier lying nearby. Now he grabbed it, tucked it under his arm, and twisted the jet control hard.

Water blasted from it in a solid silver column, striking the oncoming monster squarely through its gaping jaws. The shrieks of the beast rose in pitch, and waves of many-colored flame rippled outward along the walls and ceiling and floor. Its onslaught was slowed, but it didn't stop – and came battling on through the water stream closer, ever closer...twenty yards – fifteen yards – ten –

Then a hand, tipped with raking talons, reached out for the boy to crush him lifeless.

A hand that was as big as a door.

Chapter 24

Mark took hold of one of the Shadow's terrible fingers in a hopeless effort to push the huge hand aside: its fingernail was the size and shape of an elephant's tusk – but black and twisted and as cold as ice on a January midnight.

The face of the horror loomed over and hung above Mark, filling his field of view. Its breath was hot and foul, smelling of garbage piles and wet cellars and things dead and buried. The many eyes that gazed down upon the helpless, terrified boy were bright with torture. The roaring of the thing rose to a shattering crescendo.

Mark hardly heard the *crack* of a gun being fired above the awful din: but a hole suddenly appeared between two of the blazing red eyes – a hole that swelled and split and put forth another eye, with which to witness the teenager's dread.

The skin around the Shadow's mouth stretched and crumpled upward, and it began to laugh…

Then hands were tugging at Mark's back and shoulders, dragging him clear. A fireman in full protective clothing ran forward and swung an axe down into the beast's horny fingernail. Another of the crew smashed a door-crushing hammer onto the knuckle of the same finger, cracking the bone.

The creature bellowed and snatched its hand away, the roaring now growing loud enough to shake the ground itself, sending the firefighters off balance.

Mark had squirmed over onto his front. Now he

tried to stand, his back to the fiend. Roy was a yard away, reaching out to him. And Connor was at his shoulder, pumping more bullets into the thing's body, acting as a distraction while other teams of firefighters positioned their high-pressure hoses.

"Keep down!" Roy snapped out the command.

A second later the order was given, and the jets gushed out with the sound of a whiplash crack.

The whole world seemed to vanish in an incredible flash of the whitest light Mark could imagine. People around him yelled in amazement and confusion.

More lightning, snapping on and off – then the long, low roll of thunder that came up through the rock and the soil beneath, shaking the very souls of the people fighting for their lives.

The enraged bellowing and animal snarls of the Shadow swiftly increased in pitch until they could no longer be heard. As Mark scrambled clear, grasping for the sagging doors to the lobby, he could not resist the impulse to turn around and see for himself…

And what he saw took his breath away in a gush.

The long corridor now seemed to have tilted impossibly to become a shaft that dropped away into the infinite depths of the earth, and beyond into space.

Far below, the Shadow was falling, falling forever, its tiny limbs wriggling like an octopus sucked into a whirlpool. It became a little patch of quivering light – a piercing star at the end of the universe – a lick of red flame that lapped greedily

at the walls of the shaft –

And climbed them rapidly, hurtling toward Mark and the others.

"Get out of here!" Mark yelled at the top of his voice.

The men around him needed no telling. They dropped axes and hammers and other tools in their haste, let go of their hoses, and left them to cascade a waterfall down into the duct.

Mark was one of the last to reach the lobby. Roy and Officer Connor had stayed to assist him. Now, together, they flung themselves across the heaving lobby floor and dove out through the main doors into the chilly night.

Moments later, the flames reached the top of the shaft and burst out in a volcanic eruption of cold fire. Along the street, people ducked down as though the sky had caught fire. Great towering swirls and pillars of brilliance consumed the studio building – leaping upward to splash the boiling clouds, before subsiding once more.

The ground was churning, turning in on itself. It was drawing down the glass and bricks, the concrete and metal that had made MZTV, sucking it far underneath, out of human sight.

Threads of radiance turned the chainlink fence into a cobweb of light. Then it, too, was plucked away like a toy snatched from a child, pulled into the earth in a shower of sparkling dots that plunged into the depths.

The ground settled and lay still. There was a final rattling of stones. Then silence.

The wind died to nothing as the clouds

142

thinned and vanished like breath on a window pane. The stars came out.

And somewhere along the street, a woman wept softly because, once more, she was free.

☠

There was so much to do and say. Trying to understand what had happened would take months, Mark guessed, if not years. Many friendships would be born as the story was pieced together, carefully, bit by bit.

Ambulances were lined up at one end of Hob's Lane, while the red and blue lights from police cars flickered madly all across this part of town. Only a very few people had any idea of what had occurred this night, and Mark knew that he and Leila and Roy faced many tiring weeks of explanation.

But for now they were left alone. Tears were shed as Leila welcomed her parents and brother home. Mark also could not stop himself from sobbing as he hugged Sarah and Tina until they gasped.

Roy Case, standing a few yards away, watched his friends's happiness with a smile on his face. Sarah Watkins, seeing that he was alone, walked over toward him. Mark, and then Leila, joined them.

"I want to thank you," Sarah said softly, "for all you have done…"

"Just doing my job, ma'am," Roy chuckled. But they could all see he was pleased. She leaned forward and kissed his cheek.

"Perhaps," Sarah said, "you'd come over for dinner one evening? And Leila, you must join us, too. I'm itching to know what all of this means!"

"It'd be my pleasure," Roy said. He smiled at the teenagers fondly. "But you ought to know right away that I couldn't have done it without Leila's help, and Mark's – isn't that right, son?"

Leila and Sarah glanced at one another at Roy's use of the word. Then they looked at Mark.

And this time he didn't argue at all.